ACCIDENT WARD

GW00570754

When Nurse Joanne Marshall's boyfriend is admitted to *her* ward, she is pleased to be able to nurse him herself. But then the handsome new registrar, Paul Vincent, appears and her heart is torn in two . . .

ACCIDENT WARD

BY

CLARE LAVENHAM

MILLS & BOON LIMITED
London . Sydney . Toronto

First published in Great Britain 1981
by Mills & Boon Limited,
15–16 Brook's Mews,
London W1A 1DR

© Clare Lavenham 1981

Australian copyright 1981
Philippine copyright 1981

ISBN 0 263 73621 0

Set in Monophoto Plantin 11 on 13 pt.

Made and printed in Great Britain by
Richard Clay (The Chaucer Press) Ltd,
Bungay, Suffolk

CHAPTER ONE

THE ward was uncannily peaceful that evening. Perhaps I should have looked on it as an omen but instead of that I was glad because I wanted to get away punctually.

We had several empty beds, so there were fewer visitors than usual and they all left quietly at the proper time. For once nobody stayed behind to comment on the fact that Medway was a mixed ward.

'Downright indecent I call it, Sister!' somebody would say, or perhaps, 'Cor! Makes it worth while being in hospital when you wake up to find a blonde in the bed opposite.'

Sister Halliday would smile patiently and explain that the sexes weren't really all that mixed. The ward was a modern one with a number of rooms opening out of a central area and we didn't put men and women indiscriminately in these. But they shared the day room and the 'up' patients wandered around pretty freely.

'It works very well,' she generally ended. 'We find that most patients actually prefer it.'

Medway was a very mixed sort of ward in any case. It took patients direct from the busy

Accident Unit and consequently had a great variety of cases. Sometimes we had several on the Dangerously Ill List and then life was really hectic. Tonight, though, nobody was seriously ill and nothing prevented my prompt departure at eight o'clock.

'Certainly you can go, Nurse Marshall,' Sister said when I went to her for permission. She was a quiet woman in her mid-forties with greying hair and, in the background, a husband with multiple sclerosis. She gave me her kindly smile. 'Enjoy yourself at the party.'

'How did you know about it?' I asked in surprise.

'I can't help overhearing sometimes when my nurses are talking in the locker room with the door open. I heard Nurse Stanton telling you that another of the nurses in your set had got engaged. They share a flat, I believe?'

I confirmed that Nurse Lorna Page was now engaged and was having a party to celebrate, and Sister looked disapproving.

'Such a pity when she's only in her second year. I hope she won't think of getting married until she's passed her finals.'

'I don't know anything about her plans, Sister,' I said truthfully and then made my escape.

It was a long way to the Nurses' Home but I ran all the way there, plunged under a shower and was soon busy with my hair and make-up.

6

Not that there was much I could do about my hair; it had curled riotously all my life and there was no way I could stop it. I kept it very short and tried to ignore my friends' rude comments about its flaming red colour and the freckles that went with it.

David was frequently sarcastic about it so that sometimes I got really annoyed and told him his own head looked as if it had been thatched with new straw. He was a blue-eyed giant of a man and in his fourth year at the Thorpevale Medical School. We'd met at a rugger dance—he played for the 1st XV—and had gone around together ever since.

He was to escort me to the party tonight and, when I'd done what I could with my looks and slipped into a slinky brown-and-yellow dress in silk jersey, I went downstairs to the lounge to find him.

He wasn't there.

I knew he'd been playing in the last match of the season that afternoon but he'd assured me he would be back soon after six o'clock.

Too restless to sit down, I went out to the entrance hall and stood about impatiently. Nurses passed me all the time, either in groups or with boy friends. Every time the door opened I felt sure it must be David but it never was.

Time was flying past and my annoyance increasing. Maybe he had got late for some reason

7

and gone straight to the party? If that was the case he might at least have phoned and told me, so I'd know where I was. Really cross by now, I decided that I wouldn't wait another minute.

Elva Stanton's flat was quite near the hospital and she shared it with four other nurses. Although we were in the same set we hadn't become friendly until we were both appointed to the accident ward. Unlike me, Elva didn't have a steady boy friend but she'd been a bit mysterious lately about some male who'd entered her life and I was hoping to meet him tonight.

My heels tapping like castanets, I hurried along the street at the back of the hospital and paused at the casualty entrance as an ambulance swung past me and into the courtyard. I was just going to step off the kerb when another followed it, and behind that I could hear the approaching siren of a third.

They were going to be busy in the Unit tonight, and in the ward later on if all these casualties were admitted. Generously I spared a brief moment of pity for the poor creatures inside those three ambulances, and then hurried on towards the party.

I could hear it before I got there. The April night was warm and the windows were open, letting out a stream of music and voices into the quiet street. Luckily all the houses around were occupied by hospital people who understood

8

about parties and how you needed to let off steam to help you to cope with life and death. Nobody was likely to complain.

'Hi, Jo! Where's David then?' Elva greeted me as I entered the crowded room. She was wearing a new dress of some sort of creamy material, with a chunky red necklace and earrings to match. Her silky dark hair, entirely straight, fell softly round her shoulders and, though she wasn't pretty, she looked marvellous.

'Your guess is as good as mine,' I said curtly.

Her eyes widened. 'It's like that, is it?'

'Like what? All I know is there was no sign of him at the Nurses' Home and I didn't see why I should hang around there indefinitely and miss half the party.'

'I'm glad you didn't, though it's a bit odd, don't you think?' Without waiting for an answer she swept me into the crowd. 'You won't be lonely, that's for sure—we've got slightly more males than females at the moment.'

The large room was packed with medics, housemen and nurses, with one or two older men. I congratulated Lorna and Tony, who was a physiotherapist at the hospital, and then flung myself into an energetic dance. When I paused, breathless, someone thrust a drink into my hand.

I was hot and, badly in need of cheering up, it went down quickly. When topping up was going on I accepted a refill without a thought.

Normally I'm very careful about alcohol because I happen to be one of those unlucky people who can stand only a very little. But I was in a reckless mood that night. I'd been stood up and I didn't like it, and I wanted to forget about David. I stopped watching the door and danced slowly and sensuously with a bearded houseman from the paediatrician's team whose name I couldn't remember.

When the cassette was changed we separated and I found myself accepting another drink.

By this time warning bells were ringing loud and clear inside my head but it was too late. My eyes felt glazed and my legs didn't belong to me. I was furious with myself for being so daft and deeply ashamed too because I was the only one in such a state.

Worming my way through the crowd I reached the kitchen which was—mercifully—empty. The fire escape door instantly attracted me; I could hide out there until I felt better and no one need know what a fool I'd been.

It was deliciously cool outside and the night air was sweetly scented with wallflowers. I clutched the railing desperately and willed my extraordinary sensations to subside.

It was all David's fault. . . . If I hadn't been so annoyed with him I would have been more careful. And now the party was spoilt and that was all his fault too.

I thought back to the last few weeks. There'd been other occasions when his attitude towards our relationship hadn't come up to my expectations, but we'd patched things up and gone on.

Maybe this was the end and he'd chosen this callous way of telling me?

I didn't hear the door open behind me—I was too busy trying not to cry, though whether my tears were of anger or grief I couldn't be sure.

Suddenly a male voice said quietly, 'Are you okay? I saw you go out and wondered if you were feeling ill.'

'I—I——' Desperately embarrased, I struggled to enunciate clearly. 'I do feel a bit queer.'

There was a tiny pause and then the voice suggested, 'Perhaps some coffee would help?'

It was exactly what I needed but I tried not to sound too eager.

The door closed again and I waited, still clinging to the railing. It never even occurred to me to wonder who my rescuer might be. In my fuddled state I believed him to be a total stranger.

He returned remarkably quickly with a mug of black coffee and a crusty piece of french bread. 'Better have something to eat as well,' he advised.

'Oh no—I couldn't. I'll just have the coffee.'

'You'll eat the bread as well. Doctor's orders.'

Grimacing, I glanced up at him and for the first time it seemed to me that he was vaguely familiar. There were lighted windows all around and, in addition, the night sky was glowing with the orange illumination of the by-pass. I could see him quite clearly. Tall—though not as tall as David—dark hair fitting his head like a cap, dark eyes too.

As I drank the coffee and my mind began to clear I realised who he was. The new junior registrar on Mr Greensmith's team. I'd even got a glimmering of his name. Paul something.

'I didn't recognise you at first,' I told him as some of my self-confidence returned. Suddenly the surname floated in. 'You're Paul Vincent, aren't you? I've seen you in the ward.'

'Which ward would that be?' And when I told him it was Medway he said carelessly, 'I don't remember you.'

He sounded as though he couldn't have cared less, and though after my recent idiotic behaviour I could hardly blame him I was nevertheless a bit indignant. My tone matched his as I replied.

'I'm only a second year nurse and I don't get involved with consultants' rounds.'

That seemed to bring the conversation to a halt. I drank what remained of the coffee and ate the bread. The silence was growing uncomfortable and I suggested Paul might like to return to the party.

'Are you coming back too?' he asked.

I thought of the hot crowded room and my courage wilted. Although I felt better I was by no means completely recovered but I didn't want him to guess how bad I'd been feeling. So I said airily, 'I might as well.'

'We'll go back together.' And as an after-thought he added, 'By the way, what's your name?'

'Joanne Marshall—but my friends all call me Jo.'

'Okay, Joanne. Let's go.'

Had he meant it as a slap in the face? It certainly felt like it. I bit back a sharp retort and followed him into the kitchen.

Elva was at the sink, washing glasses and she swung round in astonishment as she heard the fire escape door.

'I wondered where on earth——' She was staring at Paul but almost immediately her gaze switched to me. 'I didn't realise *you'd* disappeared as well, Jo.'

I don't know whether it was natural thickness or because I was still a bit fuddled, but the penny took a long time to drop. When it did at last fall I realised with a jolt that Paul Vincent must be the new man in Elva's life, the one she'd been giving me dark hints about.

'I felt a bit—er—faint,' I told her. 'Paul came to see if I was all right.'

She didn't believe a word of it, that was for sure. She darted me a look of sheer hatred and then held out a tea towel to Paul. He took it in

13

silence and began to dry the glasses. I did the only thing possible and took myself off to the other room.

The party was beginning to divide up into pairs. I could see my bearded houseman weaving his way towards me and hastily joined a group which was still talking animatedly.

Suddenly there was one of those silences which happen occasionally at parties for no apparent reason. Cutting sharply through the middle of it there came the sound of the telephone.

Lorna went to answer it and we heard her say, 'I'll tell him at once ... *What?* How awful! ... More than half of them? But that's terrible!'

She re-appeared in the doorway, her eyes wide with shock, and looked round in a helpless sort of way.

'Where's Paul? He's wanted at the hospital—emergency op.'

Somebody shouted out his name and he came in from the kitchen. For the first time I really looked at him. He was certainly dishy—good features and a clear, slightly tanned skin, deep-set eyes with long lashes, and a well-shaped mouth and jutting chin. It was a pity that, judging from the arrogant tilt of his head, he believed he was God's gift to nurses.

But at the moment his mind was on the job and he asked tersely, 'Any details?'

Lorna made an effort to pull herself together

and I waited with a detached interest for her reply. I had absolutely no premonition of what it was going to mean to me.

'It's the rugger team. Their coach crashed on the way back from the match.' Suddenly she became aware of my horrified gaze. 'Oh, Joanne—that must be why David hasn't turned up——'

Somehow I galvanized my frozen limbs into life and I plunged forward and seized her by the arm. 'Did they say if anybody was badly hurt?'

She shook her head. 'You know they wouldn't tell me that. It was only because of it being our hospital team that the switchboard operator mentioned it at all.'

'I must go.'

I pushed past her, fumbled for my coat in the tiny hall and began to run down the stairs, pushing my arms into it as I went. As I reached the front door somebody caught me up. Paul.

'What does this mean to you?' He opened the door and we shot out on to the pavement. 'Have you got a boy friend in the team?'

'Yes. He was coming to the party with me and didn't turn up, but somehow I never thought——' My voice died away as I was overwhelmed by a terrible feeling of shame.

I'd never thought of anything like this as the reason for David's non-appearance. I'd taken it for granted that he'd stood me up on purpose.

How *could* I have been so self-centred?

We came to the casualty entrance and I remembered the three ambulances I'd seen. Maybe they were bringing the rugger players. If so, they would all have been examined by now and it shouldn't be difficult to find out details.

The brightly lit Accident Unit was calm. Two drunks were shouting unintelligibly and a teenager with a bleeding head was surrounded by his mates, waiting for attention. After a quick glance round Paul went through the door into the main hospital and disappeared, but I lingered to look for an opportunity to waylay one of the nurses.

We weren't supposed to visit other departments and asking questions about patients was definitely frowned on. But at that moment I cared nothing at all for rules and regulations. I was frantic with worry about David and I just had to know the truth about him.

Luckily I soon managed to corner a nurse I knew and I blurted out my question.

'There were six serious cases,' she told me, 'and ten of cuts and bruises. It was hectic in here for a time, I can tell you.'

'David Logan—you *must* remember him?' I shook her arm frantically. 'Was he one of the minor injuries?'

Her expression changed and I caught a look of pity in her eyes.

'David—well—er—no, I'm afraid he was a bit

unlucky, Jo. He got concussion and an awful lot of bruises, and—er—his right leg was badly crushed.'

'Oh, God——' I was stone cold sober now but for a moment the floor heaved like the waves of the sea.

'Sit down a minute.' She grabbed me and tried to steer me towards a chair.

'I'm okay.' I resisted her well-meant effort. 'I suppose they're operating on David tonight? Was that why Paul Vincent was sent for?'

She shook her head. 'I don't think so. He's too badly shocked. He lost rather a lot of blood, you see. But the others are being done tonight.'

'Where is he then?' I asked blankly.

'They sent him up to Medway. Isn't that your ward? Perhaps you'd be allowed to see him for a minute. It depends who's on duty.'

With a muttered word of thanks I rushed off into the hospital and up the stairs to the accident ward. Thorpevale City and General Hospital was an enormous complex, made up of old and new, but Medway was in a recently built wing not far from the Accident Unit.

Just before I reached it an idea struck me and I stopped abruptly. Surely I would stand a better chance of being let into the ward if I were in uniform? Everything, as the casualty nurse had said, depended on who was on duty, but it was worth a try. I swung round and charged down the stairs and along the covered way connecting the hospital with the Nurses' Home.

A year-and-a-half of almost daily practice had taught me to don my uniform in a few seconds. I ripped off my party dress and zipped up the well-fitting dress of small green-and-white checked material worn by student nurses. My second-year belt snapped into place and in a moment I had balanced a cap on top of my red curls. Thus clad, I set out again at a much more sedate pace.

My heart thudding, I paused in the doorway of Medway Ward. At the nurses' station in the centre a shaded light glowed warmly, but there was no one there. From all but one of the rooms round about there came the soft sound of breathing and an occasional snore.

The exception was the room nearest the door, a large one containing six beds. There were two nurses there and I saw at once that the night staff nurse was somebody new, one of the many part-timers without whom Thorpevale could not continue. She was a thin woman with short grey hair and she turned round with an anxious expression when she sensed my arrival.

Before I could speak she burst into an agitated whisper.

'I suppose you're the junior the Night Superintendent said she'd send me? Thank goodness you've come! We've got our hands full with this patient and five more will soon be here needing post-operative care.'

I saw the student nurse staring at me in aston-ishment. Shirley Brown knew perfectly well that I was on days and shouldn't have been there at all, but I managed to give her a meaningful glance before saying primly, 'What would you like me to do, Staff?'

I saw Shirley's raised eyebrows and ignored them. She wouldn't give me away, I felt sure, and I gave my full attention to what the Staff Nurse was saying.

'Sit by the patient in the first bed, Nurse, and maintain a very careful watch on him. Call me at once if you notice any change, whatever it may be. And keep an eye on that transfusion bottle.'

As I sat down by David's bed I could hardly believe my luck. I didn't give a thought to what might happen in the immediate future when my deception was discovered, as surely it was bound to be. All I cared about was that I was there, close to David, in the best possible position for discovering what the coach crash had done to him.

He lay motionless, deeply unconscious, his fair hair sticking out in tufts the way it always tended to do. There was a contusion on his right temple and the eye on that side was already turning black. One arm was bandaged from wrist to elbow and there was a cage over his legs. The tube from the blood transfusion bottle led into his undamaged arm.

My heart was bursting with grief and pity as I looked at his poor broken body. I put out my hand and touched his gently. It seemed strange to feel no response, to know that he had gone far away from me to a strange world inhabited only by himself.

He wouldn't like that, my muddled thoughts continued. He was an extrovert type, someone who loved life and people, always keen for a party, or a visit to the pub, or some violent form of exercise. Like rugger.

Would David ever play rugger again?

CHAPTER TWO

AFTER a few minutes I released David's hand and stood up to check the transfusion. When I turned round again I found someone had come up so quietly on the other side of the bed that I hadn't heard him. A man in a white coat, his dark eyes intent and serious.

For quite a while Paul stood silently by the bed, his fingers on David's wrist. Then he looked up suddenly and our eyes met.

'I thought you were supposed to be in the theatre,' I said.

'I shall be in a moment, but I wanted to check the condition of this patient first.'

He picked up the chart and studied it, and nervously I asked, 'How is he?'

'Better than he was when admitted. Not yet up to the further shock of an operation.'

'He'll be first on the list in the morning?'

'Probably.' His clinical detachment vanished suddenly. 'Am I right in assuming that your surprising appearance here is due to your emotional interest in David Logan?'

'If you're asking whether he's my boy friend,' I said curtly, 'then the answer is "yes".'

Paul hesitated and then said in a softer tone, 'Don't worry too much, Joanne. The leg fracture is a severe one—comminuted, as a matter of fact—but Mr Greensmith is a wonderful orthopaedic surgeon . . .'

'Do you think I don't know that?' I interrupted rudely.

His eyebrows lifted slightly. 'You would, of course, know his reputation better than I do, since you've been here so much longer.'

He switched his attention from me to the Staff Nurse who now came to join us.

'You'll be getting the first two patients very soon now, Staff, and the other three at intervals later on.' With another glance at me and a slight change of tone, he added, 'I'm very glad you've got a nurse to "special" this case.'

The sarcastic beast, I thought crossly as he went away. He must have guessed I'd got no right to be there. As I was again left alone with David I found myself wondering with increasing uneasiness how I was going to extricate myself from this awkward situation my own impulsiveness had led me into.

At any moment the Night Superintendent might appear and she would know at once that I wasn't what I was supposed to be. Could I disappear now and leave Staff to draw any conclusions she wished? She didn't know my name so she couldn't report me, and I didn't think

Shirley would enlighten her.

But that would mean leaving David un-attended. It was unthinkable that I should do that.

With a sigh of resignation I decided to play it by ear. If the worst happened I would have to confess all and throw myself on her mercy.

From what I knew of her she wouldn't have much.

Time passed slowly. David's pulse improved but he remained deeply unconscious. Two of the injured rugger players, both with simple frac-tures, were brought in and transferred to the beds prepared for them. I was told to keep on eye on these new arrivals.

If I hadn't been so wracked with anxiety about David and also my own possible fate, I would have enjoyed myself as I flitted silently between my three patients. I'd never had so much re-sponsibility before.

It was nearly one o'clock when the Night Superintendent paid her visit. She came in very quietly, a tall woman with a squarish face and massive bosom, and sailed towards the desk where Staff was writing busily. I felt slightly sick as I watched her.

There was a brief conversation, inaudible to me, and then the two women turned to look at me and I quailed in my seat. The staff nurse's face wore an expression of amazement mingled with reproach. Miss Jenkins looked furious.

Hastily I scrambled to my feet and clasped my shaking hands behind my back.

'What is the meaning of this, Nurse?' the Night Superintendent demanded, and never in my experience had such a quiet voice seemed so full of menace. 'I came in to tell Staff Nurse that I had been unable to send her any extra help because we are so short-staffed, and now I find *you* installed and passing yourself off as the emergency nurse supplied by me.' She paused and eyed me majestically. 'Have you any explanation to offer?'

'Please, Miss Jenkins, I didn't intend to pass myself off as anybody. I—I only came to see if I could spend a few mintues with this patient as I was very worried about him. I—er—know him quite well. The staff nurse assumed I'd been sent by you and——'

'And you made no attempt to disillusion her?'

The round grey eyes were boring into my very soul. I did my best to meet their penetrating gaze and said nervously, 'N-no—I'm afraid I didn't and, of course, I realise now I should have done so.'

Staff said anxiously, 'Nurse has been very helpful, Miss Jenkins.'

'H'm. I have never come across such extraordinary behaviour.' She stroked her chin and continued to glare at me. 'Are you on duty in the morning, Nurse?'

And when I confirmed that I was she immediately

asked how I imagined I would be able to do my work properly after sitting up half the night.

'I didn't look that far ahead,' I said truthfully.

I wasn't quite so scared now because I could see she was baffled. I'd committed a terrible crime and at the same time made myself very useful. She couldn't think what to do with me.

After keeping me in suspense for several seconds she made up her mind.

'What's your name, Nurse?' She wrote it down in a small notebook while I watched in renewed alarm. 'I must warn you to watch your behaviour very carefully in future. If there is any more of this sort of thing the consequences for you will be very grave indeed. We can't have student nurses taking it upon themselves to visit patients when they have absolutely no right to be in the ward at all. You would, after all, have seen the young man in the morning.'

I waited to learn if I was to be punished and, finding that she seemed to have finished, said hastily, 'Yes, Miss Jenkins—thank you.'

I was about to scuttle away towards the door when she made a gesture to detain me.

'Under these most exceptional circumstances, you may remain here a little longer. In about an hour's time I shall have a nurse free to take your place. But you can't possibly go on duty until lunchtime. I'll have a word with Sister Halliday.'

When she'd gone and I was back in my place,

Staff said with a tired smile, 'You're a very naughty girl to deceive me like that. I hope you realise how lucky you've been.'

I assured her fervently that I did and settled down to keep watch again. By the time I was relieved by the other nurse, the last three patients had arrived from the theatre and I was in charge of a whole roomful.

As I handed over to her I suddenly realised how tired I was. So much had happened since I set out for the party that I could not remember much of it. Had I really had too much to drink and been looked after by Paul out on the fire escape? I hadn't liked him much then and had seen no reason to change my mind when he appeared in the ward.

He must certainly have a pretty poor opinion of *me*.

Worn out by emotional strain, I tottered off to bed. But I didn't sleep much, in spite of my weariness, and would willingly have gone on duty at the normal time.

I didn't dare ring up the ward to ask how David was and it seemed an eternity before I could put in an appearance.

In the doorway I met Elva who demanded before I could speak, 'Where on earth did you get to this morning, Jo? It wasn't much fun being one short when we were so frantically busy.'

'I'll tell you another time.' I grabbed her arm. 'How's David? Did they operate?'

She shook her head. 'It was postponed until this afternoon. You'll probably be able to snatch a word with him before he's fetched.'

I was streaking off when I remembered I must report to Sister first.

She looked at me with a puzzled expression on her face when I appeared in the office.

'I've been hearing a most extraordinary report about you, Nurse Marshall.'

I said feverishly, 'Yes, Sister. I'm sorry, Sister.'

'Are you? I doubt it very much. In fact, I have a strong feeling you might do the same thing again in similar circumstances.'

There was actually a gleam of amusement in her eyes and I took heart. She, at least, understood how I felt about David.

'I don't propose to add anything to what Miss Jenkins has said to you,' Sister went on. 'But I must warn you that I shall be watching your behaviour very carefully in future, Nurse. It's most unfortunate that you're having to share in the nursing of your boy friend.' Entirely serious now, she gave me a long searching glance. 'I don't think I need say any more.'

Poised for flight, I gabbled, 'Thank you, Sister,' my mind already racing ahead to the room where David lay.

I reached his bedside at last and at first thought he was still unconscious. He'd been prepared for operation and all his tufty hair was hidden beneath a cap so that I hardly recognised him. His short fair lashes rested on cheeks which already seemed sunken, but as I leaned over him his eyes opened slowly.

'Jo!' His voice was very weak. 'Where were you this morning? I thought for sure you'd be here.'

'I—I was off duty.'

'And you never even popped in to see me——'

'We're not allowed to visit the ward——'

'I reckon they'd have made an exception in my case,' he grumbled, drawing his brows together in a frown and then wincing with pain.

'You mustn't talk too much,' I warned him.

'Why mustn't I?'

'Patients with concussion have to keep very quiet. You know that.'

'I suppose it's because of the concussion that I can't remember anything about the accident.' With an effort he raised his head and looked round the room. All the other rugger players were sitting up in bed and trying not to stare at us. 'Seems like there's nearly half the bloody team in here. Good thing it's the end of the season.'

'Yes.' I touched his hand briefly. 'I must go now, David. See you later, love.'

There was no response. Heavily sedated, he'd

already slipped away from me. Sick at heart and thoroughly dissatisfied with our conversation, I went off to do some work.

David was wheeled away to the theatre soon after that. I followed him with my eyes, longing to be with him instead of the third year nurse who walked at his side, yet relieved in a way that I hadn't been chosen for the job. I might have disgraced myself by showing my feelings.

He was gone a long, long time and we heard afterwards that he'd been kept in the recovery room for quite a while. I was obliged to fling myself into the evening rush hour without any news of him and I was glad to be so busy.

Elva summoned me to help her lift an enormously fat woman who'd fallen downstairs and damaged her back. She lay flat, a huge mound beneath the light blanket used at washing time, and it took all our strength to move her.

In the opposite bed a girl with long pale hair and a round childish face watched us anxiously.

'You'll put your own backs out if you're not careful,' she remarked.

'We *are* careful,' Elva panted. 'Learning how to lift is part of our training.'

I tucked in my side of Mrs Baxter's draw sheet and straightened up. 'So you don't think you'd like to be a nurse, Lucy?'

'I didn't say that. As a matter of fact, I used to think I might perhaps go in for nursing but then

I didn't get enough "O" levels for a proper training so I took a secretarial course instead.'

'Very sensible of you,' Elva commented.

'I didn't think that when my boss gave me a lift to work and crashed his car.' She leaned back despondently against her pillows. 'Do you think they're ever going to get my thigh set properly?'

'Of course they will. Mr Greensmith is a marvellous surgeon——' I broke off abruptly. Someone had said that to me last night—or something very like it. It had been Paul talking about David, I now remembered.

But Mr Greensmith, good as he was, couldn't work miracles. I knew he was worried about Lucy's leg because it looked like being shorter than the other, so that she would have to wear a built-up shoe.

He might have the same trouble with David. His was a worse fracture than Lucy's had been.

Hastily I collected my wandering thoughts and at the same time picked up Mrs Baxter's bowl of water. As I reached the open end of the room with it a man in a dressing-gown appeared.

'I'll empty that for you, Nurse,' he offered. 'I reckon you've got plenty to do.'

'You can say that again!' I handed him the bowl. 'Thanks, Mr Grainger.'

When I passed by a few minutes later he was still standing there, indulging in a chatting-up sort of conversation with Lucy whose curtains

had been drawn back. She was smiling and looking a bit pink and I was glad that he was apparently cheering her up.

We all liked Lucy; she was sweet-tempered and
patient, and never gave any trouble. Her fracture
had been a difficult one and I knew Mr
Greensmith was considering re-setting the femur
in the hope that she might eventually walk without a limp.

I was due to go off duty at eight o'clock and
David still hadn't come back. His parents had
arrived and were sitting silently in the waiting
room. I longed to go and talk to them but I didn't
dare after what Sister had said about watching
my behaviour.

It was the custom at Thorpevale Hospital for
two nurses in each ward to work on until ten
o'clock to help the night staff. They were, of
course, always chosen from those who had had
time off earlier in the day.

That evening, when I asked permission to
leave, Sister looked at me thoughtfully.

'I think it would be a good idea if you were to
remain on duty until ten o'clock today, Nurse
Marshall. With the ward so busy, an extra nurse
will be much appreciated.'

Never before had I so much welcomed the
chance of another two hours work. I wasn't sure
whether it was meant as a punishment or whether
she had kindly decided to give me the op-

portunity of being there when David was returned to the ward. At that moment I couldn't have cared less about her motive.

She went off duty about eight-thirty, leaving the Night Staff Nurse in charge. This was a different one, who knew nothing about the terrible crime I'd committed the previous night.

If she had, she certainly wouldn't have picked me to go and act as escort when David was pronounced fit to leave the recovery room!

My heart was thudding as I approached the quiet room next to the theatre where patients were often kept for a while after a serious operation. Only one trolley was occupied and I saw David's fair hair on the pillow. As I expected he appeared to be deeply asleep.

'He came round a couple of hours ago,' a third year nurse told me. 'He's just sleeping off the effects of the anaesthetic now.'

'How is he?' I asked tremulously.

'Fine! These rugger types are tough, you know. They can stand an awful lot.' She looked at me curiously. 'Do you know him—personally, I mean?'

'Er—yes.' I left it at that.

As I waited for a porter I studied David's unconscious face. His skin had already acquired an unfamiliar pallor but, in spite of undergoing a difficult operation, he didn't look nearly as ill as he had done last night, due entirely to the magic effects of the blood transfusion.

My spirits rose considerably as we set off for the ward. David was going to be all right . . .

When his parents came in to sit by his bedside, I looked at them with interest as I had never seen them before. Mrs Logan was a small woman with unnaturally black hair and troubled eyes. Her husband was tall like David, with the same untidy fair hair—now turning grey. Both appeared oppressed by their surroundings and acutely anxious.

'When will he be able to talk to us?' Mrs Logan asked in a whisper. 'It's awful just sitting here and saying nothing.'

'He'll be too sleepy to say much tonight, but you'll find him quite different in the morning.' I produced a bright smile and hoped I spoke the truth. 'Are you staying in Thorpevale for a few days?'

'We don't want to stay any longer than we can help because of the expense. Will David have to remain in hospital for very long? I thought they sent people home these days almost as soon as their plaster was dry.'

'It's too early to say how long he'll be hospitalised.' I added a few soothing, noncommittal remarks and went away.

I don't know whether their long wait was eventually rewarded by a little conversation with their son but when I went on duty in the morning

33

there was, of course, no sign of them.

Most of the nurses knew that David was my boy friend and it wasn't difficult for me to get the job of attending to the washing of the boys in the 'rugger room'. Most of them could manage for themselves and I was able to give my full attention to David. He still seemed to be dozing and I began to sponge his face with a warm flannel.

'Jo!' His eyes had flown open. 'For God's sake—do I have to be washed like a baby—and by you of all people?'

'Not if you feel strong enough to do it yourself' I paused and looked at him enquiringly.

His spurt of indignation had already died and he looked desperately tired.

'On second thoughts, I don't reckon I've got the energy so you might as well get on with it. There's not much of me available for washing so it won't take you long. Mind my black eye—it's hellish painful this morning.'

I sponged him very carefully and then patted him dry. He grumbled all the time but when I'd finished he caught at my hand.

'Sorry to be such a bear, Jo. I feel in a thoroughly bad mood so you'll have to make allowances.' His eyes pleaded with me for understanding.

'I'm quite willing to do that,' I said, putting the washing materials away tidily. 'I expect you're feeling the reaction after yesterday's op.'

34

'I felt fine last night, no pain and a super sort of floating-in-space sensation. Today I don't reckon there's more than an inch or two of my body that doesn't hurt.'

'You're a fourth year medic,' I reminded him briskly. 'You ought to know that the body's got to wake up and suffer for a while. I'm sure they'll give you pain-killers if it gets too bad.'

'I could do with some right now.' He gave a long weary sigh. 'I wonder how long they'll keep me in bed. The sooner I'm up and hobbling about the ward, the sooner I shall be discharged. D'you think they'll let me go back to work with the plaster on?'

'Perhaps. You'll have to wait and see.'

I'd given the only reply which seemed possible but it produced another burst of temper which made him look like a sulky schoolboy.

'For goodness sake, Jo—can't you think of anything better than that?'

'Sorry!' I bit my lip to hold back my own irritation and scolded myself internally for lack of sympathy.

During the week which followed it was often like that with David and me. Sometimes he was so bad-tempered that I almost lost patience with him, but at other times he would be apologetic and I would forgive him instantly.

Our relationship had always been stormy. We would strike sparks off each other and say things we were sorry for afterwards. But then there would be the reconciliation, so tender and sweet that I would feel it had all been worth while.

Mr Greensmith—a small man with silver hair and a young face—came daily with his retinue of registrars, housemen and medical students. They all stood round the bed, asked questions, and then went away again without anybody having any clue to the great man's thoughts.

Not that I was present on these occasions. I was generally busy doing some job in another part of the ward but David usually grumbled to me about the general lack of information.

His parents were worried, too, and they returned to London without being able to find out anything about the probable length of his time in hospital. The reason was, of course, that nobody knew.

I would have liked to ask Paul for his opinion, since he was the only one in the team I knew, but I hadn't had an opportunity of speaking to him since the evening we met. I would have been glad about that, since I didn't want to be reminded of those humiliating circumstances, if it hadn't been for wanting to know about David.

And then, one evening, the opportunity presented itself.

I was standing at the bus stop outside the hospital, on my way home to visit my parents. It had been a long, long day with a number of crises and

I was deathly tired. I also had a headache.

The weather didn't help. It was warm and airless with occasional misty rain. Everything looked as depressed as I felt.

One of these little showers arrived as I waited for my bus. I turned up the collar of my anorak and hunched my shoulders, half regretting the impulse which was sending me home on this particular evening.

It seemed as though the bus would never come. I was thinking of giving up when a smart little car in metallic blue came out of the hospital car park. It swished out on to the wet road, drove past me and then suddenly stopped and reversed. I'd never seen it before but I looked at it with a faint stirring of interest.

Maybe somebody was going to offer me a lift.

The driver leaned across and wound down the window. 'Hi Joanne! Can I offer my car as a substitute for the bus?'

I'd been wanting to see Paul, but now that he was here in front of me I hesitated. I didn't like him much; I certainly had no wish to accept favours from him.

'That depends,' I said doubtfully, 'on where you're going.'

'Anywhere. I hadn't decided. What's your destination?'

I told him I was going home and that my parents lived on the outskirts of the city in

Strawton, a village which had been swallowed up and turned into a suburb.

'But it's quite a long way from here. You have to go through the city centre and on for at least another two miles. I think I'd better wait for the bus.'

'I can go that way just as well as any other,' Paul said firmly. 'Hop in.'

I couldn't go on thinking up excuses without appearing downright rude. Besides, it was raining harder now.

And so I got in and sat in silence while Paul coped with Thorpevale's traffic. I'd wait until we got to the long straight Strawton Road, I decided, and then ask him about David. There'd be just enough time left before we reached our turning.

But it didn't work out like that at all.

CHAPTER THREE

'WHY were you setting out to drive aimlessly?' I asked when we were through the worst of the traffic.

Paul slowed down as the green light ahead turned to amber and then red. 'I thought I might learn something about the city—find my way round the one-way system and all that. But basically I suppose I needed to get away from the hospital for a while.'

'Me too.' I sighed and settled more comfortably in my seat. 'I was feeling thoroughly fraught and——'

'And everything suddenly got too much for you?' He turned his head and gave me a keen glance from his dark eyes. 'It's my guess you've got a headache too.'

I admitted that I had and was told briskly it was due to tension and I needed to unwind.

'Will that be possible at your house?'

I hesitated. 'Well—no, not really. My sister lives there—she's divorced and she's got two young children—and then Mum and Dad don't yet know about David.'

'So it would be pretty daft to go and see them

tonight, feeling the way you do at the moment. I've got a much better suggestion. How far away is the sea?'

'The *sea*?' Startled, I stared at his profile clearly outlined against the grey sky. 'About thirty miles.'

'Forty minutes driving. Let's go, shall we?'

'Go to Barhaven? But——'

'Give me one good reason why we shouldn't refresh ourselves with sea air.'

In spite of the fact that I didn't like him much, the more I thought about his idea the more attractive it seemed. I was glad when he knocked down my feeble objections like ninepins.

Luckily we were on the right side of Thorpevale for getting to the coast, and as we drove down Strawton High Street and past the road leading to my parents' house I couldn't help feeling glad I wasn't going that way after all.

'What sort of place is Barhaven?' Paul asked as we finally shook off the city and began to speed up along a dual carriageway.

'Small and quietish except in July and August. There's a short prom and a lifeboat station but no amusements.'

After that we didn't talk at all and I was already feeling relaxed when we reached Barhaven's wide shopping street, crossed it and went down a road leading to the front.

'I prescribe a brisk walk along the prom,'

Paul told me firmly.

An hour ago I would have been horrified at the idea of walking anywhere. But I was recovering so rapidly that I actually welcomed it and I set out at Paul's side with a pleasant sense of being taken in charge.

It was now quite dark and the sea was a black mass on our left, heaving gently and reflecting the town lights here and there. I remembered the last time I'd seen it, when David and I had driven over in October for a late swim. Somehow it seemed years ago, in another life, and I could hardly believe he hadn't always been lying in a hospital bed with a terribly shattered leg.

I mustn't let myself think about David. Already I could feel some of the tension returning. I made a determined effort and began to talk to Paul about Barhaven.

'I used to love coming here when I was a child. There's a small island off-shore near the far end of the prom and a causeway leading to it. I longed to be allowed to walk over at low tide but my mother would never let me in case the tide came up and I got cut off.'

'Couldn't your parents have taken you there?' Paul asked.

'Well, yes, I suppose they could but they weren't a bit adventurous. They liked to sunbathe and do a bit of swimming now and then, or just doze. And my sister always seemed to have a boy friend in tow and so she wasn't much use either.'

'I expect you've been there plenty of times since?'

'Only once or twice. There never seemed to be enough time, or else the tides didn't fit in.'

We came to the end of the promenade and halted, staring out across the sea, straining our eyes to see the line of the causeway. It was marked by tall posts but they didn't show up in the darkness.

'No good trying to go now,' Paul said. 'The tide's coming in fast.'

We stood there for some time, listening to the gentle wash of the sea and talking about the island and others like it which Paul said he'd visited. As we turned back he slipped his arm through mine and it seemed the most natural thing in the world.

The talk switched to our families. I touched briefly on my sister's broken marriage and he told me about his home. This was in a Norfolk village where his widowed mother kept a gift shop.

We were getting horribly near the car park. There were lights and raucous noises as people spilled out of a pub across the road. Two motor bikes tore past with ear-splitting acceleration.

With all my heart I longed to return to the spot where we had stood looking across at the island, and all around us there'd been only darkness and the sound of the sea.

I didn't try to analyse the feeling; I just accepted it. But there was something of it in my voice when I spoke to Paul as we reached the car.

'I can't thank you enough for this evening. I feel—totally different.'

'I've enjoyed it too,' he said quietly. 'I think we both needed a break from the hospital.'

'Yes.'

I was still looking up into his face, my gaze held by some magnetism I couldn't understand. In the harsh lighting his eyes were black and un-fathomable and his skin starkly white. There was a strained set to his lips which puzzled me.

With an abrupt movement he put both hands on my shoulders, bent his head and kissed me on the mouth. Taken by surprise, I made a muffled sound and yielded to the demanding pressure which forced my lips apart. A strange involuntary shiver passed over me.

'You're cold!' Paul released me and stepped back.

I shook my head. 'No—not really. But I think we ought to be on our way back to Thorpevale.'

'You're right there.' He laughed without much real mirth and unlocked the door.

At that moment I suddenly realised there was a couple standing quite close to us, half hidden by another car. Something made me look at them— perhaps it was because the girl was staring at me—and I met the astonished eyes of Lorna Page, one of Elva's flat mates.

Paul had noticed nothing, and probably wouldn't have recognised her anyway. He drove away from the car park in silence and we exchanged hardly a word on the homeward journey.

I worried all the way about Lorna seeing me. It would have been bad enough if she'd merely seen us together, miles from the hospital where my boy friend lay desperately injured. But what *must* she have thought of that surprising kiss?

Perhaps Paul was regretting it as much as I was, or maybe it was so unimportant to him that he hadn't given it another thought. A kiss was nothing really, just a sudden impulse, given way to and then forgotten.

'Headache better?'

We had arrived at the hospital and he was slowing down to turn into the drive. His voice was polite, formal, not at all friendly.

'Yes, thank you.' My tone matched his, or so I hoped. 'I'm very grateful to you. Some sea air was just what I needed.'

'Glad to be of use.' He parked the car neatly and got out without looking at me.

I scrambled out hastily, bumping my knee on the door, produced another spate of incoherent thanks and hurried away towards the Nurses' Home.

I suppose I'm a natural optimist; anyway,

before long I'd managed to convince myself that Lorna would soon forget about Paul and me. She might mention it to Elva, of course, but I'd soon be able to convince my friends that the expedition had been perfectly innocent.

It was therefore all the more of a shock the next day to meet Elva in the ward and discover she was in a state of seething fury.

'I never would have believed you'd behave so disgustingly, Jo! Actually to go out with another man when David is so ill—it's *horrible*!'

'I suppose Lorna told you,' I said to gain time.

'Naturally she did. She says you were embracing quite openly in the car park and he was kissing you——'

'It was only one kiss and we weren't embracing.'

'It depends how you define the word, doesn't it? What on earth were you doing out with Paul anyway?' Still accusing, she followed me to the kitchen.

I told her the story of my headache and the chance meeting, and I could see she didn't believe a word of it.

'I noticed you fancied him at the party,' she said scornfully, tipping milk so carelessly into a saucepan that it slopped over the edge.

'For your information, I did *not* fancy him then. On the contrary—I didn't like him very much.'

Elva looked so astonished I almost laughed, though I wasn't finding the situation at all funny.

'How about you fancying him *now*?' she asked nastily.

'Not even now. I have absolutely no designs on Paul Vincent. It's David I'm interested in—remember?' And I added, because I was curious, 'Does he mean an awful lot to you that you're making all this fuss?'

To my distress she went pink and tears welled up into her eyes.

'I didn't mean to say anything until I was more sure of him. We met the evening he arrived at the hospital to take up his junior registrar job. It was very late and they'd got some sort of crisis on in the kitchen and the canteen hadn't much to offer. He asked me if I knew of a pub around here that did decent bar food.'

'So you took him back to the flat and cooked him a meal——'

'No, I didn't then! I recommended the Crown and Castle, and he asked me to go along with him if I wasn't doing anything special. I wasn't and so I did—and we got on marvellously.'

'And I suppose he kissed *you* goodnight?'

'As a matter of fact, he did,' Elva told me defiantly. 'And when I invited him to Lorna's party he seemed quite keen to come. I—I thought he liked me.'

'I can't see why you've apparently concluded that all is over between you.' I tried to speak lightly. 'You might just as well accept that I

46

really did have a bad headache and he simply decided out of ordinary human kindness to do something to make it better.'

'Like kissing you at Barhaven?'

'You know I didn't mean that!' My self-control threatened to snap. 'As for the kissing, since he seems to have treated you similarly, I'm afraid we'll both have to accept that he makes a habit of it. It doesn't mean a thing.'

Elva sighed and her mouth drooped. 'Could be you're right, Jo.' She gave a yelp of dismay as her saucepan boiled over. 'Hell—what a mess!'

'What are you supposed to be doing anyway?' I asked, fetching a cloth.

'Making Horlick's for Mrs Baxter. She doesn't like coffee mid-morning.'

I remembered I was fetching orange juice for someone and hurried to get it. Even a nice sister like ours didn't approve of her nurses gossiping in the kitchen.

The juice was for one of the rugger players, who didn't like coffee either. I took it to their room and put it down on his locker. 'Thanks, love!' he said cheerfully and aimed a playful slap at my bottom. They were all—with one exception—looking fairly well now.

The exception was David.

One reason he was improving so much more slowly than the others was because he'd been so badly injured. But he shouldn't still have been running a temperature.

I paused by his bed. 'How are you feeling this morning? Better?'

'Personally I'd prefer to say I don't feel as bloody awful as I did this time last week.' He grinned ruefully. 'When d'you think they'll let me get up and hobble round a bit? Seems a pity to be in a mixed ward and not be able to take advantage of it.'

I didn't know the answer to his question and so ignored it. 'You'll have to watch your step when you're allowed up——' I broke off to laugh. 'Sorry—I didn't mean to make a joke.'

'Is that what you call it?' David went through the motions of laughing but I didn't think he was very amused.

A staff nurse at the nurses' station turned round and glared at me. She said sharply, 'Haven't you anything to do, Nurse?'

Sister would have been glad that David was even mildly cheerful but Staff Nurse Leeming was over fifty and had the most archaic ideas about the behaviour of student nurses.

I told her I was collecting coffee cups and she replied tartly that the junior could do that.

'I'm just going to start a dressing round, Nurse Marshall. You can get scrubbed up and help me.'

We worked our way slowly round the ward and came eventually to the rugger players. Their fractured limbs were in plaster but most of them had

48

lacerations which had had to be stitched, including, of course, David.

Pushing my trolley I arrived at his bedside and Staff drew the curtains. Unfortunately she turned round just in time to see the wink he gave me. Her snort of disgust sounded so funny that I had to struggle with an attack of schoolgirlish giggles.

'When you have managed to control yourself——' her tone was icy—'we will start.'

At that moment the rings on the curtains rattled and a voice said coolly, 'Excuse me, Staff. I would like a word with the patient before you begin.'

It was Paul. For all the notice he took of me I might have been a piece of hospital furniture.

Staff said huffily, 'Certainly, Doctor,' and stood back.

As David looked up enquiringly, Paul continued in the same detached tone. 'Mr Greensmith wants some more X-rays to be taken of your leg. I thought you might be surprised and wonder why if you weren't told beforehand.'

'I'm wondering now. What the hell's it in aid of?' David tilted his head and looked indignant.

'Just routine,' Paul said smoothly.

I knew perfectly well it wasn't routine. Once a surgeon has set a broken limb, provided he is satisfied, he leaves it up to nature to continue the good work unaided. With an effort I kept my eyes downcast and didn't even steal another look at David's face.

'I suppose it was a very bad fracture,' he said doubtfully.

'Yes. The radiologist will probably do it this afternoon.'

Paul disappeared through the curtains and Staff Nurse Leeming said crisply, 'Kindly undo the bandage, Nurse. I'm waiting.'

David's arm was a mess. When I removed the dressing with my forceps I caught my breath involuntarily as the red, raw cut, running from wrist to elbow, was revealed.

'Do you usually take a long time to heal?' Staff leaned forward, peering over her mask at the angry-looking stripe.

'I never thought about it.' He glanced down and grimaced.

'Well, please try and remember. When you cut your finger, for instance, do the edges draw together quickly or does it heal slowly from below?'

David flung her an impatient glance. 'I honestly haven't the faintest idea. Do you think it's this inflamed arm which is keeping my temperature up?'

'What do you know about your temperature? Have you been allowed to look at your chart?' she demanded.

'Why the hell shouldn't I? It's *my* temperature, isn't it?'

Staff gave him a long disapproving stare and didn't reply. She began to clean up the wound and David watched her in silence. When she'd finished he produced a wan smile and thanked her politely.

As soon as we were out of earshot I ventured to ask the same question which David had put to her.

She hesitated, which was most unusual with her, and her expression was troubled.

'It's possible, Nurse, that the inflammation in the patient's arm is causing his temperature to remain above normal. Personally I wouldn't have thought it bad enough for that. However, some people do run a temperature very easily, just as some take a longer time to heal than others. We shall have to wait and see.'

When I came back on duty after a free afternoon Elva told me David had had his fresh set of X-rays done.

'I don't suppose anybody's said anything about them?' I asked.

'Of course not, but maybe Sister'll tell us something at report time in the morning.'

I always tried to listen very intently when she was giving her nurses the daily report on each patient. It was important to know exactly what was going on, what sort of treatment people were getting and how they were progressing.

She'd been noncommittal about David lately,

but she did mention the X-rays the following morning.

'Mr Greensmith had to rebuild the leg completely and he was anxious to know whether he'd been successful. Of course, it's early days yet but it's important that the limb shouldn't start healing without being correctly joined.'

She went on to the next patient without telling us what the plates had revealed and my attention wandered. Afterwards I stayed behind to ask her a question. I didn't think she'd mind, since she knew about David and me.

'You want to know whether the operation was successful, Nurse?' Sister paused, studying my face. 'Well, I'm afraid the X-rays were not entirely satisfactory. However, Mr Greensmith is still hopeful.' She smiled and dismissed me before I could ask how much they'd told David.

I was relieved to find that he knew as much as I did but his attitude towards the information was entirely different. Just because Mr Greensmith was considered such a wonderful surgeon he was taking it for granted that everything would eventually turn out all right.

'It looks like being a very long-drawn-out affair, Jo.' He held my hand tightly beneath the bedclothes when I went to say goodnight before going off duty. 'I suppose I've just got to learn to be patient but it won't be easy for me.'

'No,' I agreed. 'You're not the patient type any more than I am.'

'I'm sorry I get bad-tempered so often.'

David rarely apologised for anything and I was touched at this new and humble mood.

'Don't give it a thought,' I told him. 'I'm used to bad-tempered patients.'

'That could have been more tactfully put!'

We both laughed and he kissed my hand swiftly and returned it to me.

But as I left the ward I felt far from happy. It seemed strange that I, a natural optimist, found it so hard to be optimistic about David's leg.

CHAPTER FOUR

THE population of Medway was constantly changing. During the next few days two of the rugger players were discharged and Mrs Baxter was fitted with a steel corset and allowed to go home.

Her bed was immediately occupied by a girl named Cheryll who'd been knocked off her moped by somebody opening a car door carelessly. She wasn't much hurt and during the short time she stayed with us she was allowed to wander about the ward more or less as she liked.

'I wish I was free to move around like Cheryll,' Lucy said wistfully. 'So far I've only been allowed to sit by my bed and that's not much fun. I might just as well be in it.'

'It's better for you to sit in a chair for a while.' I finished making her bed ready for her return and smoothed the bedspread. 'For one thing you're less likely to get bedsores.'

'I suppose so.' As she didn't know how horrible bed sores can be, she wasn't very impressed. 'Other people with broken legs are able to walk about with a sort of half hoop under the foot. Nobody's ever suggested I should have one.' She gazed at me with her large blue eyes. 'Why is that, Nurse?'

I struggled to think of an answer which would satisfy her and failed to come up with anything except a vague, 'Well, your fracture was a very difficult one, you see. There are several different kinds of fractures and——'

'That poor David Logan must have had a bad one too,' she interrupted. 'Have they let him walk about yet?'

'Goodness, no! He hasn't been out of bed at all. You're luckier than he is.'

'But I had my accident at least a week earlier. I ought to be further advanced.'

She wasn't usually as depressed as this and I felt concerned about her. Lingering to chat—it was Staff Nurse Leeming's day off—I asked if she was expecting any visitors that afternoon.

'Only Mum—she comes every day, and I get visitors most evenings too. I'm very lucky.' She sighed, hesitated and then suddenly revealed the real reason for her black mood. 'I wish my boy friend would come more often. I've got an awful feeling he—he——' Tears filled her eyes.

'Yes?' I asked gently. 'What's this feeling you've got?'

'That—that he doesn't want to be bothered with me any more. As soon as he discovered I would have a long convalescence he just didn't want to know. I don't think he's got much use for a girl friend who's sort of out of reach, if you know what I mean.'

'It must be very frustrating,' I agreed, and I thought of David and myself.

We'd already experienced the difficulties of a similar situation, with the added complication of my being a nurse who had to watch her behaviour with a patient.

I was tempted to tell Lucy that I had problems too but I thought it might be better for her to get her own troubles off her chest if she felt like it. This seemed to be the case; now she'd got started she didn't want to stop talking about her unsatisfactory boy friend.

'Simon hasn't been to see me for three whole days. I'm not sure now that he really loves me at all though I thought he did before the accident. In fact——' she went slightly pink—'he'd been trying to persuade me to leave home and move into his flat. I think I might have given in if this hadn't happened.'

I remembered Simon—a bit over-weight with a black moustache, not my type at all, and I could just imagine he wouldn't care much for having a girl friend he couldn't make passionate love to.

'If he's really gone off you because of the accident,' I said briskly, 'then it seems to me he's not much loss. You must be very glad you didn't leave home because of him.'

'Yes, I suppose I am.' She produced another

long-drawn-out sigh. 'It would certainly have been terribly humiliating to have him cool off after we'd been everything to each other.'

I moved away, amused at her old-fashioned expressions and deeply sorry for her at the same time. She was the only child of elderly parents and her slightly out-of-date air and fragile appearance made her very attractive to men. I didn't think she'd have much trouble finding another boy friend when she was better.

But, in the meantime, there was the problem of her leg. On the morning following our conversation Mr Greensmith made up his mind to re-set it.

Afterwards I found her in tears.

'I'm right back to square one,' she sobbed. 'All this time I've been in hospital has been wasted.'

I did my best to comfort her but I wasn't very successful. Later on I told David about her, even though we weren't supposed to gossip about one patient to another.

He was also sunk in gloom that morning after a bad night with a good deal of pain. He complained that the plaster on his leg was killing him. I didn't think he paid much attention when I was talking about Lucy but he did manage to express sympathy.

'Poor kid,' he said when I'd finished. 'I hope for her sake she's not going through the hell that I am at this moment.'

'I don't think she's actually in pain,' I was obliged to admit, 'but if Mr Greensmith doesn't do something she'll have one leg shorter than the other and have to wear a built-up shoe.'

'I suppose that would be pretty hard to take, specially for a girl.' A look of alarm crossed his face. 'Jo—you don't think that's likely to happen to me, do you? *I* shan't end up with one leg a different length?'

I hastened to reassure him. 'Nobody's ever suggested such a possibility——'

'But they might have discussed it among themselves. Nobody ever tells the patient anything, as you'll discover if you're ever unlucky enough to become one.' His tone became more aggrieved. 'You'd think they'd treat me differently, seeing I'm a medic myself, but they don't. It's still all hush-hush.'

He made a grab for my hand and clutched it feverishly. 'Do they say anything about me when Sister gives the nurses the daily report? I see you all standing round that desk affair and I can't hear a damn word.'

'You're not supposed to,' I told him and then wished I'd had the sense to put it differently. David immediately assumed I really did have secret knowledge.

'Come on, Jo—let me into the secret!' he begged.

'There isn't any secret. Sister only tells us

about the drugs patients are on, and what sort of night they've had. You don't need me to tell you you had a bad one, that's for sure.'

'Like hell, I don't!' he agreed.

There were a dozen things I ought to be doing and I was obliged to tug my hand away from his clasp and leave him. I did so with the certain knowledge that my well-meant attempt to cheer him up had been a dismal failure.

By this time I was feeling depressed myself, and as I later went off for my coffee break the old childish wish popped into my head, 'If only something *nice* would happen——'

You don't often get those sort of wishes granted but it happened to me that morning and in the most unexpected way.

I was sitting in the canteen staring glumly into my mug of coffee when Paul appeared and asked if he could join me. Since I'd been wanting someone to talk to, I welcomed him in a way that Elva certainly wouldn't have approved of.

'I wanted to see you, Joanne.' He took a sip and looked at me briefly across the table. 'The thing is, I'm trying to make up a small party to go to a dance on Saturday week. I wondered if you were free.'

I looked down to hide my astonishment and thought rapidly but I couldn't remember my duties so far ahead.

'I'm not sure, Paul, but perhaps it could be

fixed. Tell me more—where is this dance and who's going to it?'

'It's a charity ball, actually, at a house about twenty miles from here. As a matter of fact—' he seemed slightly embarrassed '—my aunt lives there and she always sends me half-a-dozen free tickets but I'm not always working near enough to make it. This year it should be quite easy.'

'So it's an annual affair?'

'Yes, in aid of the Red Cross.'

'Your aunt must have a very large house,' I couldn't help commenting.

'Er—well, yes. She lives at Letherington Hall. Her husband made a packet in industry and was clever enough to get out while the going was good. Financially she's way above the rest of the family but it hasn't affected her attitude.'

'I should hope not,' I said loftily.

Paul's eyebrows lifted. 'Be your age, Joanne! Money can make the hell of a lot of difference.'

I said I supposed it could though I wasn't likely to get any personal experience of the problem. 'Who's included in this party, Paul?'

'Elva for one, and her flat mate Lorna, and Lorna's fiancé. I forget his name——'

'Tony.' I counted up the names and made it five. Somehow my initial enthusiasm seemed to be evaporating. 'Who am I going to be paired off with?'

'Elva suggested Robert Curtis, one of the house-men on our team.'

'*Elva* suggested him?' I was indignant at not being consulted. 'I've got nothing against Robert. In fact, I doubt very much whether anybody could have—there's nothing either to like or dislike.'

'That's why he seemed so suitable,' Paul explained calmly.

'Meaning?'

'Elva didn't think your boy friend would mind you going with anybody so—er—harmless.'

I was sick of having Elva quoted at me but I managed to control my annoyance. In spite of the dullness of my prospective partner I was still pleased at being included. Just to go to Letherington Hall as a guest would be fun; nothing like that had ever happened to me before.

'We'll all mix up anyway,' Paul said, 'so you won't get stuck with Robert the whole evening.' His gaze held mine for a moment. 'You'll let me know as soon as possible if you can't fix it?' And when I assured him that I would, he added softly, 'I hope very much that you will be able to come, Joanne.'

Obviously he didn't want the bother of finding another girl. I could understand that and I quickly dismissed the crazy idea that he might want me to come for my own sake.

Back in the ward I went at once to consult the

61

duty rota and discovered to my joy that Saturday week was one of those days when I finished at five o'clock. Elva hadn't been so lucky; she should have worked until eight but her name was scratched out and another nurse's substituted.

I supposed I ought to say something about the dance. When we met in the locker room before going off duty I tossed off a casual remark, saying I was surprised at being invited.

'Have I got you to thank for including me?' I asked.

Elva hesitated and I could see she wished I hadn't put that particular question.

'Well, actually it was Paul who suggested you. He doesn't know many people, not having been here very long. He remembered you and I and Lorna were friends,' she went on, rallying quickly, 'and so he thought it would be nice for us to get together.' Her eyes sparkled. 'I'm looking forward to it enormously, aren't you?'

'So-so,' I said carelessly, but I couldn't help adding, 'I've never been to a really grand affair before. Imagine living in a house with a ball-room!'

'It sounds a super place. Paul told me quite a lot about it. And Lady Farnham must be nice because he seems so fond of her.'

'*Lady* Farnham? Is that his aunt?' I stared at her in amazement.

'Yes, of course. Didn't you know her name?

It's not an old title—I expect her husband bought his knighthood in some way—but the house is seventeenth century and it stands in a huge park. Paul used to stay there sometimes when he was a medical student.'

'He's certainly put you thoroughly in the picture,' I said grudgingly.

Elva was looking in the mirror and I saw her preen herself.

'He talks to me quite a bit.'

I wondered *when* Paul talked to her and supposed it must be at the flat. But it was no concern of mine. Resolutely I concentrated on wondering what I was going to wear.

Several things happened in the ward during the intervening time. Lucy had her leg re-set and shed her depression as soon as she'd got over the op. A school bus got involved in an accident near the hospital and we had an influx of twelve-and thirteen-year-olds with minor injuries. They only stayed two or three days but they turned Medway into a bear garden while they were there.

David's condition continued to give anxiety. His temperature refused to return to normal in spite of the antibiotics he was receiving. He constantly complained of pain.

I dreaded telling him I was going out to enjoy myself on the Saturday evening. It might have been kinder not to mention it but I couldn't bring myself to do that. I was already feeling quite guilty enough.

Unfortunately I didn't choose my moment very well. In order to have a private conversation with him I had to fit it in with what was going on in the ward. It was impossible to fit in with David's mood too.

In any case, I didn't know his leg was hurting him even more than usual.

'You what?' His over-bright eyes stared into mine. 'That's great, that is! I'm lying here on a bed of pain and you're off to spend the evening with another bloke. I didn't think you were that sort of girl, Jo.'

'I'm *not*!' I was getting angry too but I clung to my temper. 'And I'm not spending the evening with another bloke. There'll be three of them and I was definitely told there wouldn't be any pairing off, except with Lorna and Tony. I wouldn't stand for it anyway.'

'Who are the other two blokes?' David demanded.

'You know them both.' I told him who they were. 'I'm not in the least attracted to either of them.'

As I spoke I remembered that evening by the sea with Paul which had ended so surprisingly. Though I'd disliked him so much at first there was no denying I'd felt differently since then.

To my relief David appeared somewhat mol-

lified. 'Deadly dull, both of them. You'll probably be bored to death.'

'Could be—but at least I shall enjoy
Letherington Hall, I hope. There's a famous
band and the food ought to be good.'

'It'll probably be a stuffed shirt sort of affair.
Not your kind of do at all. How come you were
invited?'

'Something to do with Elva and Lorna and I all
being friends.' And I added carelessly, 'Elva
rather fancies Paul, I think.'

'I don't care who she fancies so long as you
remember you're *my* girl.' He pressed a kiss on
the back of my hand. 'God!—how much longer is
it going to be before I can kiss you properly?'

'Not long, I hope.' As I wriggled my hand free
I could still feel the burning imprint of his lips.

David made no further reference to the ball
until Saturday afternoon, just before I went off
duty. Then, as I was whisking past his bed
during the evening toilet round, he called out to
me.

'I'm not going to say I hope you enjoy yourself
tonight, Jo, because it wouldn't be true.'

'Thanks very much!' Natural as his attitude
was, it narked me a bit. 'I suppose you're hoping
to hear in the morning that I loathed every
minute?'

'You needn't go as far as that.' He smiled
wryly. 'Just tell me you were bored and all the

time wishing I was there, and I'll be satisfied.'

'I'll do my best,' I promised.

I'd pretended to take it lightly because David had spoken that way, but I knew perfectly well that underneath he was in earnest. He *really* didn't want me to enjoy myself.

I was still brooding over it as I lay in a scented bath piled high with bubbles of foam. Then it occurred to me that maybe I ought to be glad David wasn't pretending. If he'd put on an act and made out he didn't care about my going out, I might have wondered whether it was for real.

My muddled thoughts were getting me more and more bogged down and, with a sudden upsurge of good spirits, I jettisoned the lot. I must look my best tonight and that was going to take a great deal of concentration.

My make-up took ages but I was satisfied with the result. I couldn't do anything with my hair, of course. It would never hang in a silken curtain like Elva's, or touch my shoulders with the ends curled under like Lorna wore hers. All I could do was brush it until it shone and let it settle itself the way it wanted to, which meant that a childish curl flopped down over my eyes.

When I'd lacquered it back again I slipped into the new dress I'd splashed out on for the occasion. It was made of a soft silky material which draped beautifully and the sea-green colour suited me. I smoothed it down over my hips and hoped Lady Farnham wouldn't disapprove of the plunge neckline.

David would have appreciated it. He loved to slide his hands inside my sweater and cup my breasts in his palms. As I remembered the effect of his touch a sudden sensuous shiver passed over my body. For a moment I wished desperately that the accident had never happened and I was going to the ball with him and no one else.

Once more I put David out of my mind and I picked up my velvet cloak and went downstairs to wait for the others.

It seemed somehow a bit strange to get in the back of Paul's car, where Robert greeted me cheerfully, and see Elva installed in the front seat. Last time I'd ridden in this car, *I* had occupied the front.

Robert was saying something and I jerked my attention back to him.

'Are you good at ballroom dancing, Jo?' he was asking. 'I'm afraid I'm not.'

'I haven't done any since I was at dancing class—ages ago. But I reckon we'll manage.'

It didn't take long to get to Letherington Hall and it turned out to be even more imposing than I had pictured it. We entered the park through wrought iron gates picked out with gold paint, and followed a long drive which wound its way past belts of huge trees.

When the house came into view it looked enormous—a great block of masonry standing four storeys high and with a lot of ornamentation along the edge of the roof. There was a porch with a wide flight of steps leading up to it and the great door stood wide open. Although it wasn't quite dark, light streamed from nearly every window.

The right-hand end was obviously the ballroom. It had very long windows with crimson velvet curtains looped back and we could see people dancing.

'I'm afraid you'll find a lot of older people present,' Paul warned as we got out. 'It's one of the social events of the year and the local people come.'

'I don't mind.' Elva gazed up into his face and slipped her arm in his in a very proprietary sort of way. 'I'm just so thrilled to be here.'

As we turned towards the steps Robert slouched along at my side with his hands in his pockets and his eyes on the two in front.

'They seem very interested in each other,' he observed. 'I don't think we shall see much of them tonight. What with that and Tony and Lorna being engaged, we shall have to make the best of each other, Jo.' And he laughed uproariously as though he'd made a good joke.

But it didn't seem all that funny to me.

CHAPTER FIVE

WHEN we entered the hall we found our host and hostess waiting to greet their guests, just as if it had been a private party and not a money-raising affair. Lady Farnham was tall and dark, like Paul, and most beautifully dressed in silver and black, but Sir Michael was a little round man with a bald head and a red face already shining with sweat.

Paul's aunt kissed him affectionately and shook hands with the rest of us, while her husband, speaking in a strong north country accent, told us to enjoy ourselves.

'There's plenty of good food, so don't stint yourselves. I only wish I could indulge——' he patted his protruding stomach. 'Plenty of booze, too, and champagne for those that like it. Personally I don't think you can beat a nice glass of real ale.'

Our homely welcome had dispelled the slight awe which our grand surroundings had induced. We went down a wide corridor, hung with paintings, and separated to the rooms prepared as cloakrooms. When we met in the ballroom it was already half full and the band was playing a quick step.

Lorna and Tony passed and waved and Elva turned to Paul. 'Come on, let's make the most of this. We can do some of our own steps to this tempo.'

They went off together and I glanced at Robert. 'Shall we try it too?'

'If you're prepared to risk it.' He took hold of me uncertainly and held me a good four inches from his chest.

We began to move jerkily more or less in time with the music. Every now and then Robert trod on my foot and apologised, and after we'd made two complete circuits of the room without any improvement I suggested we should sit down.

'I'm sorry, Jo,' he muttered. 'I guess I'm not used to dancing and holding a girl at the same time. At the hospital discos you're on your own and it's fine, but here——!' Words failed him.

'I wouldn't have thought having me in your arms would put you so much off your stride,' I teased.

'It's not that.' The idiot had taken me literally. 'I don't seem to be able to fit my steps to someone else's—see?'

I could see very clearly that I was in for a dull evening. Lorna and Tony weren't likely to split up to rescue me from Robert and there didn't seem much hope that Elva and Paul would do so either. She wouldn't have forgotten that time

70

when he'd taken me to Barhaven and she wouldn't want to run any risks—or what she might imagine to be risks.

Until then I'd enjoyed just being at Letherington Hall, but now I looked round the ballroom at the middle-aged couples doing their old-fashioned steps and a great wave of longing for a disco came over me. Robert wasn't the only one who would feel more at home there.

I'd looked forward to the evening so much and bought the new dress for it, and nobody had even mentioned it. Tears of disappointment filled my eyes and I winked them away angrily. Robert wasn't particularly perceptive but even he would notice if his partner suddenly cried all over him.

We sat there watching the dancing for a while and the ballroom began to fill up. A lot of younger people arrived and the band changed its tempo, playing alternate dances to please both groups of people. This was much better; Robert and I could join in and my drooping spirits revived.

At the end of a particularly energetic dance we found the other four had joined us.

'How about some supper before it gets too crowded?' Paul suggested.

We all followed him to another huge room where there was a buffet laden with gorgeous food: fresh salmon, cold turkey, ham and lots of delicious salads, trifles, mousses and cheese-

71

cakes, fresh fruit and an enormous cheeseboard.

There was a vacant table which would take six and we settled down at it. I was between Robert and Tony and opposite Paul, which meant I could witness all Elva's possessive little ways.

Like everyone else I had a glass of wine, and when the waitress came round to top up our glasses I got mine re-filled with the others.

Two glasses—it was my ration and I was absolutely determined not to drink any more.

Towards the end of the delicious meal she came round again and this time I put my hand over the glass.

'What on earth's got into you, Jo?' Robert had noticed the gesture. He lowered his voice. 'Don't you know it's free? Make the most of it and don't be daft!'

'I've had all I want, thanks,' I said quietly.

But he was already calling the waitress back. 'The young lady's changed her mind.'

The others were looking at me and I removed my hand hastily. I'd let her fill up my glass but nobody could make me drink it. As for Robert, I was absolutely furious with him.

'Will you kindly mind your own business!' I hissed at him.

'I don't know what you're so annoyed about,' he told me in an injured tone.

'You made me feel conspicuous and I don't like it.'

'Sorry!'

I could see he was honestly bewildered and he'd certainly meant no harm, and so I struggled to subdue my irritation. But I didn't drink the wine.

When we'd all eaten as much as we could manage, Robert glared at my full glass.

'You're surely not going to waste it, Jo! After all the trouble I took too.'

I looked at him and shrugged. 'I told you I didn't want it.'

'Go on, Jo,' Lorna put in. 'I can't think why you're making such a fuss.'

Elva said nothing. She knew about my unfortunate reaction to alcohol and I guessed she was trying not to make matters worse.

But Tony had had his own glass filled several times and was in that happy state when the silliest things seem uproariously funny.

'Let's make Jo sit there until she's drunk her wine.' He beamed round the table, delighted with himself and his good idea. 'Like our mothers used to do when we were kids. "You can't get down until you've finished your porridge" and all that. So drink up, Jo, there's a good girl, if you want to go and do some more dancing.'

All this time, Paul had taken no part in the conversation but now he exploded into it with a force that made everybody stare at him.

'For God's sake—shut up, Tony—and you too, Robert! It's up to Jo how much she drinks and there's no need for anybody else to comment. Shall we go back to the ballroom?'

We trailed behind him in silence. Although I was grateful for his support I wished it hadn't been necessary.

'What on earth made Paul sound off like that?' Robert grumbled.

'He just happened to know I don't drink much, that's all. And now, if you don't mind, the subject is closed,' I snapped.

'Okay, okay.' He surveyed the crowded ballroom and made an exclamation of disgust. 'Another of those old-fashioned dances! A waltz, isn't it? I'm afraid that's utterly beyond me.'

'I wouldn't dream of attempting it with you.' I sat down on the nearest chair.

And then, quite suddenly, I found Paul standing in front of me and holding out his arms.

'It's time we broke up a bit. I expect you can waltz, Joanne?'

I told him I could and we moved off together. I fielded a disgusted look from Elva before she turned to Tony, leaving Lorna stuck with Robert, but I didn't care. Before long I forgot everything, even my annoyance over the wine, and just gave myself up to the pleasure of waltzing with a really good dancer.

With half-closed eyes I allowed the dreamy music to waft me along on waves of bliss. It seemed like Paul and I were one, our bodies moving in perfect unity, and I wished the dance would go on for ever and ever.

It had to end eventually, of course. As I reluctantly came back to reality I realised we hadn't spoken one word to each other the whole time.

But now Paul was looking down at me and smiling. 'Thank you. That was wonderful.'

I said sedately, 'I enjoyed it too, very much.'

'I'm sorry you've had so much of Robert's company. He's a nice lad but a rotten dancer. I didn't know he was quite so hopeless.'

'Most boys are. They don't have much chance to learn ballroom dancing.' I looked up at him. 'How come you're so good?'

'My aunt insisted on my learning when I was staying here. It's like swimming and riding a bike—something you don't forget.'

We were standing at the far end of the ballroom, right away from the rest of our party, and Paul made no move to join them. I glanced round at the beautiful room, lit by glittering chandeliers; the gleaming parquet floor and the masses of hothouse flowers along the edge of the dais all spoke of wealth.

'I simply can't imagine what it's like to stay at a place like this. You're very lucky to have such rich relations.'

But Paul shook his head. 'It isn't because of the money that I'm lucky—or, at least, only partly. It's because they're nice and I like them.'

'Well, of course, that's important too' I

thought of my own family and discovered to my surprise that the ones I liked best were those with least money. All the same, I wasn't so naïve as to imagine money didn't count. 'You seem to have been lucky all round,' I told Paul.

He raised his eyebrows slightly. 'Maybe—I haven't thought about it much. Changing the subject, Joanne, would you like to see round the house since you're taking such an interest in it?'

'Oh, Paul—I'd *adore* it! But will your aunt mind? It seems an awful cheek——'

'Of course she won't mind. She's very proud of her house and likes people to admire it.' He seized my arm. 'Come on, let's get away before the others find us.'

He made straight for a door I hadn't noticed and suddenly we were outside on the terrace. The night breeze was deliciously cool and a huge bush of white lilac filled the air with its intoxicating scent.

'It's quicker this way,' Paul explained. 'You're not cold?'

'I don't feel I could ever be cold again.'

The touch of his hand on my bare arm had set my veins on fire. As we strolled past the long windows of the ballroom I wished the terrace would go on for ever so I could drink in the sweetness of the night until my senses could absorb no more.

'It's lovely out here,' Paul said.

'Yes.'

'Seems a shame to go in.'

I didn't answer and a moment later we came to the front door, which still stood open. The hall was empty now and no one would have known if we'd just glanced in and then continued into the park.

I could feel that Paul was hesitating. I knew I only had to suggest walking a little further and he would have agreed. But I didn't dare. There was a magic in the air which, coming so soon after that slow sensuous waltz, I couldn't fight.

'Come on,' I said abruptly. 'I thought you were going to show me the house.'

He followed me in without a word and we stared up at the stags' heads on the panelled walls. Higher up still there was a sort of gallery which was reached by the beautiful curving staircase.

Paul opened a door on the left and showed me a long drawing room with a moulded ceiling and furniture covered in pink brocade.

'They don't use this much—it's too big.' He turned down a corridor. 'This is the dining room—and that's too big as well.'

It was huge and gloomy, with paintings round the walls and an enormous table. I much preferred the morning room where Paul said they usually had their meals. This was a cheerful room, with comfortable chairs, even a little worn, and an ordinary-sized table.

The library was lovely—cool and dignified—

but as I admired the rows and rows of books I was told they'd been bought only for their bindings.

'They're never taken out and read, but the room does get used because my uncle has made it into his study.' Paul looked down at me. 'Like to see upstairs, or have you had enough?'

I said I could never stare enough at how well-heeled people lived and I'd certainly never get another chance. 'But I don't think you ought to take me upstairs, Paul. It's sort of more private somehow.'

'There's no reason why I shouldn't show you the main guest room. It's got a fourposter bed and is nearly big enough to hold a ball in—well, a disco anyway.'

We went up the stairs hand-in-hand and somehow it seemed so natural I hardly noticed it. The gallery went round on three sides with corridors opening off it, and just inside one of these Paul flung a door open and switched on a whole galaxy of lights. I blinked and took a step forward, my feet sinking into the carpet.

The fourposter bed was draped with blue velvet curtains embroidered in silver, and the dressing table was laden with crystal and silver, all sparkling in the lights. There were two armchairs, a small table and numerous other items of furniture. A white-painted door led to a magnificent bathroom.

'There's a wonderful view of the park in day-light.' Paul crossed to the window and I followed him. We stood there, side-by-side, staring out at the dark scene, and suddenly I heard a bird trying out a few trilling notes. Its song was taken up by another and another.

Nightingales. It was all it needed and my heart was so full I almost choked.

'That's a real bonus.' Paul put his arm across my shoulders. I tried to speak and couldn't.

We were silent for a moment and then he asked, 'Did you tell David you were coming here tonight?'

'Of course I did! It wouldn't have been fair not to.'

'Didn't he mind?'

I hesitated. 'Well, yes, he wasn't too keen but I pointed out it was something special I didn't want to miss.' I began to improvise. 'I'm sure he understood that it was the chance of a lifetime and that made him feel differently about it.'

'I'm glad he didn't try to stop you coming.'

'So am I—I've enjoyed it so much.'

As I spoke it occurred to me that I hadn't exactly enjoyed the first part of the evening but somehow the happiness of the past half-hour had wiped out my memories of that.

'I'm glad,' Paul said simply.

This time the silence lasted for quite a while. We gazed out at the dark trees outlined against a paler sky, listening to the nightingales and watching a very young moon entangled in wispy cloud.

I was very much aware of the weight and warmth of Paul's hand on my shoulder. His fingers were resting on my bare flesh again and moving with a gentle caressing touch, and suddenly I was aware of a desperate longing to have him slide both hands inside my dress, the way David used to do.

David . . . I mustn't forget him—I mustn't! He would be furiously angry—and rightly—if he knew I was here with Paul, and in a bedroom of all places.

I moved uneasily. 'We ought to go back. The others will wonder where we are.'

'Let them wonder,' Paul said lightly. 'We aren't doing any harm.'

'N-no, of course not, but——' I made a more determined effort to evade his arm. 'I really think we ought to go, Paul.'

'In a minute. But first I'm going to kiss you. And you needn't feel you're being disloyal to David because I'm doing it entirely for my own pleasure.' He drew me closer and I didn't even try to resist. 'You look so sweet in that dress. It goes perfectly with your green eyes and those ridiculous red curls.'

His lips were on mine and their hard pressure was such sweet happiness that I trembled in his arms. Sheer weakness kept me a prisoner for a

moment and then I somehow found the strength
to break away.

'No—you mustn't! It's not fair——' I pushed
against his chest with my hands.

Paul released me at once. 'You're perfectly
right, Joanne—it's not fair. I don't know what
came over me.' He was breathing hard and his
eyes were distressed. 'But you mustn't blame
yourself in any way. As I told you, I wanted to
kiss you and I did it, and it wasn't your fault.
You've absolutely no reason to feel guilty.'

'I—I can't help it.' I put both hands over my
face and turned my back on him.

'You're crying! Is it because of me? I wouldn't
have that happen for the world.'

'I'm not crying.' I swallowed down an enormous lump in my throat but my eyes were quite
dry. 'I feel ashamed.'

'But I told you—you've no need to feel anything of the sort. It was entirely my fault.'

'No, it wasn't.' I turned round and faced him,
much calmer now. 'It was the general set-up.
This lovely house and the nightingales and the
view over the park and—and everything. I guess
we both got carried away. The important thing is
that we should realise it *was* all just sugar-sweet
and frothy and not important.' And I repeated
firmly, '*Not in the least important.*'

For several seconds Paul held my gaze and
somehow I managed to face him without shrink-

ing. Then he shrugged and swung away towards the door.

'You're perfectly right, Joanne. I'm sorry I tried to build it up into something that mattered. The best thing we can both do is forget about it as quickly as possible. Shall we go back to the ballroom?'

As I trailed after him down the stairs I felt as flat and empty as a pricked balloon. I could hardly believe that my mood had been so different only fifteen minutes ago. Then I had trodden on air, borne along on a magic cloud of false emotion, and now I wondered how I was going to be able to face the rest of the evening.

Our return to the ballroom couldn't have been better stage-managed. The band was playing a modern number and all the young people, and some of the older ones, were doing their own thing. Paul and I flung ourselves into it and gradually let the crush of dancers separate us.

When I glimpsed him later he was dancing opposite Elva. Her dark hair was flying out round her head and she looked radiant, so perhaps she hadn't realised that he and I had disappeared together.

After a while I found Robert, energetically performing in a corner. He, too, seemed to have noticed nothing and I couldn't help feeling Paul and I had been luckier than we deserved.

Gradually the effects of that strange interlude

wore off. Once more I tried to make the best of my unsatisfactory partner; after all, he was quite nice really and unaccountably my heart warmed towards him.

It didn't bother me when he put his arm round me in the car going home. I even rested my head on his shoulder. None of it was of the slightest importance.

I'd said that to Paul, I remembered, and he'd appeared to believe me. All the same, I didn't think it would be a good idea for us to be alone together again—not ever. I daren't risk a repeat of that crazy emotion which had swept me off my feet.

And as I accepted Robert's casual goodnight kiss, I reminded myself that it was *David* whom I truly loved—David, who now needed me more than ever before.

CHAPTER SIX

IN the morning I was free until lunchtime and could have a long lie-in. When I reached the ward there was the usual slightly relaxed Sunday atmosphere. Consultants didn't make their rounds at the weekend and we'd had no new admissions.

The first person I saw was Elva.

'Lucky you, having the morning off!' she greeted me. 'I went to sleep again after the alarm and didn't get any breakfast as a result.'

'We weren't all that late last night,' I pointed out. 'The dance finished before midnight because of it being Sunday the next day. I was in bed before one.'

'Well, of course, you and Robert were the first to be dropped off, since you both live in.' Elva looked at me with a small secret smile playing round her lips. 'When we got to the flat Paul came in for coffee and that made it *a lot* later.'

I dug my nails into my palms, aghast at the hatred I felt for my friend at that moment.

'Has anything interesting happened in the ward since yesterday?' I asked, deliberately changing the subject.

She shook her head. 'It's been uncannily

quiet.' Her face changed. 'They seem more than ever worried about David. His parents were ages in Sister's office this morning, talking about him. They both looked terribly distressed.'

Mr and Mrs Logan always came down from London at the weekends and I thought how disappointing it must be for them never to find him looking better.

I went to speak to them as soon as they came back to the ward after lunch and found them sitting by David's bed. Mrs Logan seemed smaller than ever and, in spite of her black hair, she looked quite old. Her husband hadn't changed much except that his shoulders were slightly bowed.

David was asleep and I spoke almost in a whisper, asking how they were and saying what a chilly day it was, and all the inane things you do say when you're trying to steer clear of emotion.

'We're as well as can be expected,' Mrs Logan told me. She lowered her voice still further. 'We did hope there'd be good news of David this week but I can't help feeling they've made a right mess of his leg.'

'Now, dear,' her husband admonished her, 'it's not fair to blame the surgeon. It was the accident which made a mess of it, not him.'

'How do you know that? You haven't any medical knowledge. Jo—' she appealed to me '—is it true what they keep telling us, that this

Mr Greensmith is good at his job?'

'It really is true,' I assured her.

'It's hard to believe. I keep wondering if we oughtn't to insist on a second opinion.'

'You could do that, of course, but——'

She cut me off in mid-sentence. 'Come over here, Jo—I want to talk to you and I daren't risk David waking up and hearing.' Casting an anguished glance over her shoulder at his unconscious face, she towed me away towards the great expanse of glass which filled the end of the room.

There was a wide view of roofs and chimney pots, tower blocks and the spire of the cathedral but neither of us looked at it.

'I told the Sister that we wanted to speak to Mr Greensmith about David and she got busy on the phone and fixed up for him to come to the hospital this afternoon. I suppose it's good of him really,' she added grudgingly, 'seeing as it's a Sunday.'

'Well, surgeons work very long hours during the week and they do like to keep Sundays free. But, on the other hand, they prefer the next-of-kin to be kept in the picture.'

If only I could stop talking in platitudes and become human . . . Surely I was as distressed about David as anybody? Mrs Logan must be finding my manner as starched as my apron.

And then—just for a fleeting moment—I remembered the last time I'd stood at a window staring out. Last night, with Paul. That must be why I couldn't behave naturally; I was still feeling guilty.

'I don't like that expression "next-of-kin",' Mrs Logan was saying. 'It sounds—well, you know what I mean.'

I knew only too well and wished I hadn't used it. I hastily explained that it was just a useful hospital expression and constantly on our lips.

She gave a long sigh and her mouth drooped. 'It's silly, isn't it—I wanted so badly to talk to Mr Greensmith but when he agreed to come without making any fuss I immediately began to wonder what he'd got to say to us. D'you think there's anything that we don't already know?'

As I answered her question to the best of my ability I felt thankful that I had no inside knowledge and didn't have to conceal anything. People in an acute state of anxiety about those dear to them have a heightened perception which often makes them realise when they're being deceived.

Sunday afternoon proceeded along the usual lines. The patients were awakened from their naps and made tidy for their visitors. Before long people were pouring in—always more on Sunday—bearing flowers and fruit and clean laundry. There was a babble of conversation and a general air of jollity.

Tea was served and then cleared away. As I helped the orderly push her enormous trolley out to the kitchen, Sister appeared and beckoned to me.

'Will you tell Mr and Mrs Logan that Mr Greensmith is in my office, please?'

I looked quickly at her face but, although she looked serious, I could detect nothing out of the ordinary. Just as I was going off to do her errand she called out to me.

'Make a pot of fresh tea, Nurse, and bring it in after about ten minutes.'

I assumed that she wanted to give the surgeon some tea and looked at my watch to make a note of the time. I would have preferred to give the message to Mr and Mrs Logan without David hearing but he was wide awake now.

They went off, looking nervous, and David moved restlessly in his bed, wincing with pain.

'Is it very uncomfortable this afternoon?' I put my fingers on his wrist.

'No more than it was this morning, or yesterday evening while you were enjoying yourself at the ball,' he said sulkily. 'I suppose you *did* enjoy it?'

It was the first time he'd mentioned it.

'I enjoyed seeing inside such a gorgeous house, and the food was super. But I didn't find Robert a very inspiring partner.'

David instantly pounced on that innocent remark. 'I thought you said there wasn't going to be any pairing off?'

'I only repeated to you what I was told, but I suppose it was inevitable with Lorna and Tony being engaged and Elva definitely interested in Paul. I wasn't "paired off" with Robert—I just got stuck with him. He's terribly boring and he can't do ballroom dancing.'

'Neither can I,' David reminded me.

'You wouldn't have been as bad as he was,' I assured him with conviction. 'After he'd stood on my foot for the umpteenth time we gave up and only did the modern stuff.'

'Did he kiss you goodnight?'

'I hardly noticed.' I decided on a downright lie. 'No, he didn't.'

'Not even an ordinary meaningless goodnight kiss?' he persisted.

'Not even that.'

Once more I crushed the memory of those crazy few minutes in Lady Farnham's guest room. There'd been nothing ordinary or meaningless about *Paul*'s kiss. It had been easy to lie about Robert—I'd done it entirely for David's sake—but I knew that if he'd chosen to challenge me concerning Paul I could never have convinced him that nothing had happened.

David closed his eyes and lay back against the pillows. 'Why have my parents gone to talk to Mr Greensmith?'

'Didn't they tell you?' I improvised rapidly. 'They never have a chance to talk to him during the week and I expect they feel cut off. It's only natural.'

'I feel cut off too—from everything that matters most to me. All my ordinary life—the Medical School and rugger and going to the pub—every blooming thing. You most of all, Jo,' he added hastily.

'You're actually seeing a lot more of me than you do normally,' I pointed out. 'Except when I'm off duty I'm around all day and every day.' I suddenly noticed the time. 'I must fly! Sister gave me a job to do.'

Luckily we had a fast-boiling electric kettle and the tea was soon made. I was waiting for it to brew and putting the cups on a tray when Paul came into the kitchen.

'Who's getting VIP treatment?' He looked at my preparations.

'Mr Greensmith and the Logans.' My voice sounded strained and unnatural and I found it impossible to face him. 'Do you want a cup of tea? I can spare you some.'

'Thanks.'

He was standing close to me and a little to one side. With every fibre of my being I was aware of him but he didn't seem to be conscious of me in any special way; both his expression and his voice were oddly detached.

I poured out five cups of tea and put one on the kitchen table. As I was picking up my tray

Paul said quietly, 'I wonder what the boss will tell them.'

'What do you mean?' I was jerked right out of my absorption in my own strange sensations and looked straight at him without embarrassment. 'They already know it was a difficult fracture and isn't setting too well. What else is there to say?'

Paul hesitated and then lowered his voice. 'You'd better prepare yourself for a shock, Jo.'

'For goodness sake!' I was exasperated. 'I'm a nurse—remember? I'm not a next-of-kin, liable to faint. What are you trying to tell me?'

'It's possible that the leg will *never* be okay. David may have to face life with permanent damage.'

'Oh, God—that's awful! You mean he's going to be a—a cripple?' I stared at Paul blankly.

'I didn't say so definitely. I said it was possible.'

I tried to think of David walking with a stick—for ever and ever. David, who was so athletic. His splendid physique had been one of the reasons I was originally attracted to him. I found myself hoping that Mr Greensmith would be very guarded indeed in what he told the Logans.

We were both silent for a moment and then Paul said, 'Hadn't you better take that tea in before it gets cold?'

I was nervous when I tapped on the office door

but Sister's voice sounded the same as usual and I found no atmosphere of uncontrolled emotion. Mrs Logan's eyes were wet and her husband looked stricken, so I guessed Mr Greensmith had been fairly frank, but they both took a cup of tea and thanked me politely.

Suddenly Mrs Logan burst into speech. 'Perhaps you don't know, Sister, that this is David's girl friend——'

'I did know actually.' Her eyes met mine for a moment.

'Don't you think she ought to be told the bad news? I know she'll probably hear about it with the other nurses some time but it seems cruel not to tell her privately, so to speak.'

As I listened I felt appalled. Was it even worse than Paul had suggested?

Sister looked at me thoughtfully and seemed to make up her mind. Mr Greensmith turned his back and stared out of the window. I took a deep breath and prepared myself to react convincingly. They mustn't guess I'd been warned.

'In spite of every effort,' Sister began quietly, 'it has proved impossible to set David's leg satisfactorily and it's not just a case of trying again—as with another patient in the ward. Mr Greensmith has already done everything that *can* be done.'

She went on and on, using a lot of words and giving me plenty of time to adjust to the information. I was grateful to her—and even more grateful when she finished without saying anything more than Paul had done.

It was bad enough. But I knew it might have been even worse.

'So our David'll be a cripple?' Mrs Logan said sadly.

Mr Greensmith turned round. 'I would prefer to say that it's unlikely he will regain *full* use of his leg.'

'It doesn't make much difference what you call it.'

'Now, now, dear.' Mr Logan roused himself with an effort. 'I'm sure we're very grateful for Mr Greensmith's kindness in giving up his Sunday afternoon to talk to us. I just wish he'd had better news, that's all.'

'We all wish that,' Sister said with a sigh. She glanced at me. 'Leave the cups here, Nurse, and come back for them later.' She dismissed me with a nod and I escaped.

I went straight to the locker room and burst into tears. Most of all I cried for David and the blow which must fall on him, but I cried for myself as well because of the dark future which loomed up in front of me too. Would I be able to give David the love and support he was going to need?

Did I love him enough?

As I returned to the ward after re-doing my face, I suddenly realised that another question was clamouring for attention. How much would they tell David?

I had no chance of finding out just then because Sister followed me in and beckoned me.

'We've got five new cases coming in soon. There's been a pile-up on the ring road. Get a junior to help you and start making up the beds.'

'Male or female, Sister?' I asked.

'Three women and two men. You'll have to move beds around to accommodate them but it shouldn't be too difficult.' On the point of turning away, she added, 'There's a married couple among them. Put them near each other if possible.'

She'd given me quite a problem which was perhaps her intention. I mentally reviewed our patients and decided that the couple could go in one of the smaller rooms where the other two patients, although both male, were well enough to spend all their time in the day room. With curtains partly drawn it would be private enough for the new woman patient unless she was the prudish type.

Sister approved my suggestion and we began pushing beds about. We were just ready when the first trolley arrived. The occupant turned out to be a Mrs Tupman, the patient whose comfort we'd been concerning ourselves with. Her face and head were badly lacerated and bruised but otherwise she wasn't hurt.

'I wasn't wearing my seat belt and I went through the windscreen. It was terrifying!' Her eyes, wide with remembered horror, stared into mine.

'You were lucky not to get any fractures.' I began to make out her chart.

'My husband broke his clavicle. That's the collar bone, isn't it? He's in the theatre now, having it set. Shall I be able to see him when he comes to the ward?'

I smiled into her anxious face. 'He's being put in the bed opposite so you should get a good view of him.'

'Really?' She could hardly believe it. 'I knew this was a mixed ward but I didn't think—well, I mean, it's a bit unusual, isn't it?'

'We often get husbands and wives, since this is an accident ward, and they mostly appreciate being near each other.' I explained about the two male patients in the same room. 'You won't mind? They're nice boys and you'll hardly see them.'

'I shan't let it worry me. All I really care about is having Bill handy so I can keep an eye on him. He didn't come off as lightly as me.'

By the time all the new patients had arrived and been accommodated it was visiting hour again, and I still hadn't had a chance to go near David. Had he heard Mr Greensmith's verdict on his leg yet?

His parents always left early in the evening as the Sunday trains weren't very frequent. He would be alone now.

But he wasn't alone. Lucy was sitting beside his bed.

I knew they were acquainted because now that she was mobile she'd got friendly with nearly everyone in the ward, but I was surprised to find her talking to David at visiting time. She always had so many people to see her.

'Hi, Lucy!' I approached the bed on the other side and automatically straightened the covers. 'How come you're not surrounded by visitors this evening?'

'Nobody turned up.' She smiled and grimaced. 'I expect I've been here too long—my friends are fed up with coming. And Mum and Dad have both got awful colds. They wouldn't want to risk bringing me germs.'

'I'm sure your friends aren't fed up—I expect it was just one of those things. Everybody happened to have something else they had to do.' I glanced at David and tried to judge from his expression what mood he was in. He was looking remarkably relaxed and I decided that one of his pain-killing injections was just taking effect.

'Anyway,' I went on cheerfully, 'it was nice for David to have you to talk to after his parents left.'

'Lucy's been telling me about her office,' he put in. 'Sounds like a loony-bin to me. I reckon

96

ARE YOU A FAN OF
MILLS & BOON
DOCTOR-NURSE ROMANCES?

IF YOU are a regular United Kingdom reader of Mills & Boon
Doctor-Nurse Romances you might like to tell us your
opinion of the books we publish to help us in publishing the
books *you* like.

Mills & Boon are planning to set up a Reader Panel for
Doctor-Nurse readers. Each person on the Panel will receive
a questionnaire every third month asking you for *your*
opinion of the past six Doctor-Nurse books. All people who
send in their replies will have a chance of winning a FREE
year's supply of Doctor-Nurse romances.

IF YOU would like to be considered for inclusion on the Panel
please give us details about yourself below. We can't
guarantee that everyone will be on the Panel but first come
will be first considered. All postage will be free.

Age -24 □ 25-34 □ 35-44 □ 45-54 □ 55-64 □ 65+ □

Age at completion of full-time education . . . .

Single □ Married □ Widowed □ Divorced □

If any children at home their ages please . . . .

Your name (print please) . . . .

Address . . . .

. . . .

Post code . . . .

THANK YOU! PLEASE TEAR OUT AND POST
NO STAMP NEEDED IN THE U.K.

DR0581/RD

she ought to change her job when she's fit again.'

'I probably will. I feel like making a completely fresh start.' Lucy stood up and gathered her pale blue dressing-gown round her. Her long fine hair hung down on both sides of her small face like a shining curtain of pure gold. Her lovely eyes were full of compassion but all she said was, ''Bye for now, David. See you tomorrow.'

'She's a nice child,' I said when she'd hobbled away.

David looked surprised. 'She didn't strike me as all that young.'

I thought for a moment and realised Lucy was a year older than me, but it certainly didn't feel that way.

'She's got a very sensible way of looking at things,' David went on. 'I told her what Mr Greensmith had said about my leg——' Noticing my start of surprise, he said defiantly, 'Any reason why I shouldn't?'

'N-no, of course not,' I agreed hastily. 'What did she say which struck you as so sensible?'

He seemed a little embarrassed. 'It sounds a bit daft when you repeat it. What she pointed out was that Nature is a lot cleverer than orthopaedic surgeons and might even now find a way of healing my leg so that I could use it fairly normally.'

I received the statement with secret dismay. Lucy had meant well, I was sure of that, but it hardly seemed kind to bolster up David's hopes.

Mr Greensmith had been so very definite in his opinion.

'I'm glad she's cheered you up anyway,' I said evasively. 'I was afraid——' I broke off abruptly.

'You were afraid you'd find me sobbing my heart out?'

'Not that, but I thought you might be—depressed.'

'Well, I wasn't exactly in a cheerful mood for a while, though I tried to put on an act for the parents' sake. Then Sister turned up and said I'd been ordered a different kind of injection. She didn't tell me what it was—needless to say! Ever since then I've had a rather pleasant floating feeling. I was just in the right frame of mind to listen to Lucy going on and on about people I'd never heard of.'

I left him lying with his eyes half closed. Whatever he'd been given must have been pretty strong.

As I returned to the new patients I was puzzled. Was it because of the sedative that David had found Lucy so appealing? He could so easily have been thoroughly irritated by her naïvety and might even have been very rude.

I didn't know what to think.

CHAPTER SEVEN

'THIS ward is getting just like a bed and breakfast place,' Elva complained as she whipped off the bedding from a newly vacated bed and began to get it ready for the next arrival. 'D'you know that Mrs Tupman actually told me she was enjoying being in hospital!'

'Why shouldn't she?' I tucked in my side of the bed. 'I reckon it's a nice rest for busy housewives provided they aren't feeling too bad.'

We were working opposite David, who was regarding us morosely. The magical effect of the new drug he'd been given on Sunday hadn't lasted long and it seemed to me that his black moods were becoming more and more frequent.

'Who am I going to be lumbered with now?' he called across to us.

'A motor cyclist who came off his bike at the London Road roundabout. His girl friend was hurt too and she's going in with Lucy.'

'Bad cases?' he asked with some show of interest.

'Not the girl. I think the boy's rather more knocked about.' I straightened up. 'You'll be able to find out when he arrives.'

Brian and Sandra were brought in soon after

our conversation. The girl came first, her eye make-up smudged and a great swelling on her forehead. She was concussed and very confused and would have to be kept very quiet for a few days.

Brian had a fractured arm and one of his legs was in an awful mess but not broken. He also had two damaged ribs and complained constantly because it hurt him to breathe.

'Can't you shut that bloke up?' David asked wearily.

'He's had a pain-killer,' I told him. 'I expect it'll start to take effect soon.'

They both slept soundly during the afternoon. David was having bad nights and so we always let him sleep if possible, but no patient was ever allowed to miss a meal because of napping, even when it was only tea.

Accordingly, around three o'clock, I approached his bed and roused him gently.

'What the hell d'you want, Jo?' He opened his eyes and glared at me.

'Just to make you comfy for tea.' I started to sort out his pillows.

I suppose it was daft of me to use that childish word but nurses do tend to talk down to their patients sometimes. I could hardly have chosen a worse patient to talk down to than David.

'What do you think I am? A kid in a bloody high chair?' His sunken eyes blazed. 'For God's sake go away and leave me to finish my nap.'

'But tea will be here in a minute——'

'I don't want any. I'm not hungry.' He shut his eyes tightly and burrowed into the pillow.

I sighed and straightened the covers. I was just moving the bed table into position when Staff Nurse Leeming bore down on me.

'Really, Nurse—don't you even now know how to make a patient comfortable for eating and drinking? David can't possibly manage in that position.' She moved to the other side of the bed. 'I'll help you raise him.'

I waited in trepidation for the storm of protest, but it didn't come. David merely heaved an exhausted sigh and collapsed against his newly arranged pillows. I had to conclude that his display of temper had been specially for me.

When I went to the locker room to take off my apron before going for my own tea I met Elva just returning from having hers.

She gave me a sharp look and said, 'Anyone'd think you were carrying all the worries of the ward on your shoulders. What's up?'

'Only David being difficult—as usual.'

'I don't see why you can't just take it for granted. I mean, it's only natural he should be in a filthy temper after what's happened.'

She was resettling her cap on top of the neat roll in which she wore her hair when in uniform. Our eyes met in the mirror and she looked reproachful. 'It's going to mean a great deal to David having his girl friend stick by him,' Elva was saying earnestly. 'I really do think you ought to be more patient with him, Jo.'

'I wish you'd tell me something I don't already know!' I flung at her and rushed out of the room and downstairs to the canteen.

I was sitting by myself at a small table and staring into space while my tea cooled. A voice spoke from behind me.

'Mind if I join you?'

Paul was still in his green theatre gown, with his hair all untidy after he'd dragged the cap off. I guessed he'd slipped out for a cuppa between operations.

'You look as though you could do with something stronger than tea,' I said, noticing the weary smudges beneath his eyes.

He sat down and leaned his elbows on the table. 'It's been quite a day, and nowhere near finished yet. I've been in the theatre since nine o'clock.'

'No lunch?'

'No.' He looked without enthusiasm at a ham sandwich on his plate. 'I think I'm past it now.'

'Better eat it,' I advised.

Paul smiled faintly. 'Okay, Nurse, I'll do my best.' He took a reluctant bite and chewed it. 'How are things in Medway?'

'Busy.'

'That motor cyclist settled down yet? He was in a blue funk before his arm was set.'

We went on talking spasmodically. It was the first time that conversation had laboured from one to the other with such difficulty. At Barhaven we had talked easily and naturally, and on other occasions too—but I tried not to think of those.

Suddenly Paul mentioned David.

'I'm afraid Mr Greensmith's gloomy prognosis was a great blow to him. He's taking it badly.'

'Surely that's perfectly natural,' I snapped, remembering what Elva had said.

He looked surprised at my reaction. 'It must make things very difficult for you. I expect he wants a lot of—of tenderness from his girl friend and yet you've got to watch your step with Sister. It's a complex situation.'

'Do you think I don't know that?' I crashed my cup into its saucer and stood up. 'Elva was going on at me a few minutes ago and neither of you has said anything I'm not fully aware of. I—I——' My voice trembled and I stopped abruptly.

Paul looked up at me, and his dark eyes captured my gaze and held it. 'Any time you need to let off steam I'd be glad to lend a listening ear—though not in the canteen perhaps!' He hesitated. 'I could also offer a shoulder to cry on if that would help.'

'Thank you.' Because I was in urgent need of the latter I spoke extra formally. 'You—you're very kind. And now I must go. As you reminded me, I need to watch my step on the ward just now and I can't afford to be late back.'

It was the most unsatisfactory conversation I'd had with Paul for a long time and yet he hadn't said anything that wasn't sensible and true. What—in heaven's name—did I want him to say?

I left the question unanswered and plunged back into work. Luckily we were really busy for a few days and I had every excuse for not giving David as much of my attention as he thought he ought to have.

Brian, fortunately, had stopped moaning but he was now annoying David even more by having his girl friend practically in bed with him. Sandra was mobile and she spent all day with her boy friend, unless turned out by the nurses. Theoretically she merely sat by his side but they managed to get themselves so entwined that David declared they made him feel nauseated.

'How much longer is she going to be here, Jo?' he demanded. 'It's obvious there's nothing much wrong with her.'

'I think she'll probably be discharged tomorrow.'

'Thank God for that! It's a pity he's not going too.'

I didn't take much notice of the remark then, but after a day or two I found myself echoing it.

Brian, bored after Sandra's departure, decided to take an interest in me.

He'd grab hold of my arm every time I went near him and run his fingers up and down it. Sometimes he startled me by pinching my bottom so that I squeaked out loud before I could stop myself.

'Keep your hands to yourself!' I flashed.

'Cor—you haven't got red hair for nothing!' He gazed admiringly at my curls. 'Come on, darling—be nice to me. I always did fancy girls with your colouring.'

I suppose I should have complained to Sister but I was so ashamed of not being able to handle the situation myself that I kept quiet about it. Staff Nurse Leeming had an inkling, of course, but she thought it was all my fault for being too familiar with the patients.

David had a grandstand view of Brian's efforts to get my attention but at first he didn't take much notice. Then, for some reason, he decided to be jealous. Unfortunately my tormentor was wildly good-looking, with thick longish brown hair, tawny eyes and positively film-star features.

It all came to a climax one evening when Brian suddenly grabbed a handful of my apron and tugged so that I almost overbalanced on top of him. His undamaged arm held me in a vice-like grip and he was grinning as though it was the biggest joke in the world.

'Let me go!' I almost slapped his face.

'Not till you give me a kiss.'

'I shouldn't dream of kissing you—not here or anywhere else.'

'Why wouldn't you?' His pride was hurt. 'Aren't I good enough for you? Most of the girls fancy me no end.'

'Don't be silly.' I tried to be scornful and dignified but it wasn't easy with my face scarlet and my cap awry. 'Please let me go——'

It was at this point that David intervened.

'Cut it out, mate,' he said wearily. 'I object to seeing my girl being pawed by another bloke.'

'You can't stop me,' Brian jeered.

David went as white as paper and I held my breath for the storm to break.

'You're a dirty fighter, aren't you?' he said between his teeth. 'You know darned well I can't stop you, but if I could—' his voice was rising '—I'd give you such a thrashing you'd never mess about with someone else's girl ever again.'

It was at this precise moment that Staff Nurse Leeming, attracted by angry voices, put in an appearance.

'What on earth is going on here?' she demanded angrily. 'Nurse Marshall, will you come away from that patient at once!'

Brian, recognising the voice of authority, immediately released me, but I don't suppose she realised that—until then—I literally hadn't been able to escape.

Staff went up to David's bed and spoke to him much more gently. 'There's no need for you to upset yourself over this. No doubt it was only a bit of—er—horseplay.'

'Horseplay be damned!' David exploded. 'That chap's been making a pass at Jo ever since Sandra went home. I don't see why I should stand for it.'

'There's certainly no need for you to do so.' She looked me up and down contemptuously. 'Go and tidy yourself, Nurse, and then come and speak to me.'

Sister was off duty so I was at Staff Nurse Leeming's mercy. My hair combed and my cap straight, I presented myself for slaughter. For fully fifteen seconds she looked me up and down slowly, as though searching for something she could find fault with. I stood very straight with my hands behind my back but inwardly I was wilting.

'I just don't understand you, Nurse,' she said at last. 'That you should actually encourage a boy of Brian's type right in front of someone to whom you are practically engaged is quite byond my comprehension.'

'I've *never* encouraged him——' I began passionately.

'A boy like that needs very little to make him imagine he is attractive to a girl. You should have been doubly careful, particularly in view of the special circumstances. I'm afraid your young man has been seriously upset at a time when he requires a great deal of patience and understanding.'

'The last thing I want is to upset, David——' I tried again and once more I was interrupted.

'Really, Nurse?' She raised scanty eyebrows. 'I find that rather difficult to accept——'

It was my turn to break in. 'And I'm not practically engaged to him. We never thought about the future. He was just my boy friend, that's all.'

'Well, of course, I don't pretend to understand the way you young people go on. But one thing I am quite sure of is that there must be no more of this flirting with Brian. It's most unseemly conduct in a nurse. You could be in serious trouble if it was reported to a Senior Nursing Officer.'

I looked at her in horror. 'You wouldn't do that, Staff!'

She shrugged. 'It's not my place to do so, but I shall feel obliged to mention your conduct to Sister. She will do what she thinks best.'

She gave me a nod of dismissal and I walked away absolutely seething. It wasn't fair, I told myself passionately—I'd never done anything to make Brian think I even tolerated him and yet Staff had actually accused me of flirting.

It was the last straw to find David inclined to share her opinion.

'Did you get an awful ticking off from that dried up old spinster?' he asked when I went to say goodnight to him.

Even though I had my back turned I could *feel* Brian's cheeky grin aimed in my direction. I lowered my voice and spoke resentfully.

'She wouldn't believe it wasn't partly my own fault and it isn't fair——'

'Well, maybe you could have been firmer with him right at the start,' David said. 'It didn't look to me as though you were trying hard enough to make him see there was nothing doing. You can't wonder he didn't get the message.'

'You really believe that?' I demanded in outrage, scarcely able to believe my ears.

'I've seen the whole thing, haven't I? I reckon you ought to have slapped the bloke's face the first time he tried something on, Jo.'

'Nurses don't slap patients' faces. Supposing he'd complained about me? I would have been in even worse trouble.'

David leaned back and yawned wearily. 'Okay, okay, you've made your point and now let's give it a rest, shall we?'

I didn't want to. I longed to thrash it out until I'd *made* him see my point of view but somehow I managed to keep a hold on my temper.

'I'd better go,' I said tautly.

'What are your hours tomorrow?' he asked languidly.

'It's my day off.' And I couldn't help adding fervently, 'Thank goodness!'

As I went across to the Nurses' Home I wondered what to do with my free day. Perhaps if the weather was good and the tide was right I might take the bus to Barhaven and walk out to the island. It wouldn't be much fun alone but at least it would get me right away from the hospital. The way I was feeling just then I badly needed to do something completely different.

But in the morning the weather wasn't at all cooperative. It was dull and cool, with a threat of rain. Instead of going to Barhaven I decided to mooch round the shops and perhaps buy myself something new.

I was wandering through the shopping precinct, looking for a summer dress I could afford, when I met my sister.

'Mum was saying we hadn't seen you for ages.' Sue looked at me accusingly. 'Had you forgotten you have a home and family?'

'Not really, but life's been a bit hectic lately.' I evaded her eyes. 'Perhaps I'll come along later today.'

Sue was taller than me, with straight sandy hair which she wore tied back. She had on jeans and a sloppy blouse and I thought she was looking shabby and fed up.

'Can you spare the time to help me choose a dress?' I asked impulsively.

'I'd rather choose one for myself.' She smiled ruefully. 'But funds won't run to it, I'm afraid. Okay, Jo—I'll give you the benefit of my advice.'

We spent an interesting hour together and I managed to find an Indian cotton dress I could just about afford. Then I went home with her for lunch.

My two little nieces greeted me shyly and I felt guilty because I saw so little of them. It wasn't that I didn't love them but since I'd become a nurse I seemed to find the noise and chaos of home life wasn't what I needed during my off duty time.

But somehow today was different. I slipped easily into the familiar background and even felt reluctant when the time came to leave.

It was only nine o'clock but my father had strong views about girls being out alone in a big city after dark.

'You hear of such terrible things happening,' he reminded me. 'It's disgraceful that a girl isn't safe out on her own any more. I'll walk to the bus stop with you, Jo, and you'll be able to get off quite close to the Nurses' Home.'

I didn't argue because it wasn't worth it, but when I reached the hospital it still seemed too early to go in. On an impulse I decided to go along to the flat and see if Elva was there.

There were no sounds coming from it though the window was open and I was afraid everybody was out. However, I thought I'd ring the bell to make sure.

Nothing happened for a moment and then I heard a faint noise from within. The lock turned and Elva stood there, looking very attractive in a gaily embroidered caftan and her hair hanging loose.

'Jo! What on earth do you want?' She stared at me in astonishment.

It wasn't the greeting I'd hoped for and I said hastily, 'Nothing actually—unless you've got any coffee going? I—er—just called on the off chance of finding somebody at home.'

'They're all out except me.' She tossed back her hair and gave me a very odd look. 'Paul's here, by the way. He also dropped in for coffee.'

CHAPTER EIGHT

'PAUL!' I gazed at Elva blankly and then turned to flee. 'I'm sorry—I didn't know——'

'How should you?' To my surprise she put out a hand to detain me. 'We've just made coffee, as a matter of fact, so you might as well come in and have some.'

I was puzzled by the invitation until it occurred to me that she could hardly turn me away coffee-less since we were supposed to be friends. And also that she might have a sense of triumph in displaying her relationship with Paul to me.

But I was still reluctant. 'It really doesn't matter,' I protested.

'I can't think why you're making such a fuss,' Elva said. 'If you want some coffee, come and have it, and if you don't why did you bother to call anyway?'

'I just felt sociable.' But I let her take me into the tiny hall without further protest, un-comfortably conscious that my hesitation wouldn't be easy to explain, even to myself.

Paul was sitting on the settee and he rose pol-itely as I came in, apparently as astonished to see me as I'd been to hear of his presence.

I hadn't spoken to him since our conversation in the canteen, when he'd offered me a shoulder to cry on. The memory of it was vivid in my mind but I could detect no sign of anything more than a very casual friendliness in his greeting.

I sat down in one of the shabby armchairs while Elva fetched a tray from the kitchen and put it on a low table in front of the settee. It was pretty clear from a squashed cushion that she'd been sitting there, very close to Paul, a moment ago.

I wished more than ever that I hadn't come.

Elva chattered cheerfully as she handed out the mugs of coffee, mostly about things that had happened in the ward that day. I was glad to hear that I'd missed the admission of a particularly nasty burns case.

'She was only twelve and she'd been frying chips for the family while Mum was at work. Somehow the fat got too hot and burst into flames, and she tried to put it out by pouring water on it. You can guess the result.'

I said I'd rather not. 'Is she staying in Medway?'

Elva nodded. 'We've put her in that little room we keep for such cases. She's too old for the children's ward.'

We went on talking about burns and how sickening we found them. Paul said he was glad he was on an orthopaedic team and didn't have to cope with them.

'You get horrible things in the orthopaedic world too,' Elva pointed out. 'Amputations, for instance.'

'I haven't had much experience of those, thank goodness.'

We were silent for a moment and then I asked how David was.

'I wondered when you were going to mention him,' Elva said nastily. 'I thought he seemed a bit better. Didn't you, Paul?'

'Doctors don't get the same opportunities of observing the patients' progress as nurses.' He took a sip of coffee and put the mug down. 'If they're going on all right we probably only see them once a day but nurses can take in every change, however slight. Ward sisters, of course, know more about it than anybody.'

I wondered why he was being so stiff. He almost sounded as though he were addressing a class of students. Perhaps my arrival had embarrassed him? If so, he wouldn't have to be troubled with my presence much longer, and as soon as I'd gone he and Elva could carry on as before.

As soon as my mug was empty I stood up to go.

Elva didn't make any attempt to dissuade me but, to my surprise and confusion, Paul also rose to his feet.

'I guess I'll be going along too, Elva. Thanks a lot for the hospitality.' And to me he added, 'Maybe you'd be glad of an escort between here and the hospital.'

'But it's no distance—honestly! I shall be quite all right,' I stammered. 'I've walked it hundreds of times by myself.'

'So have I,' Elva put in furiously. 'You're being perfectly ridiculous, Paul—I can't think what's come over you. The road is well lit and I'm perfectly certain Jo isn't in the least scared.' She glanced at the clock. 'It's only half-past ten!'

I suddenly remembered my father's care for my safety a little earlier that evening. Two men—both anxious to protect me from the dangers of the city after dark! As far as my father was concerned, perhaps it was only natural, but I couldn't believe Paul was really seriously worried about me.

Could it be that he wanted to get away from the flat?

But that didn't make sense either, since he had apparently called there voluntarily.

I gave it up and decided I'd better accept gracefully—but not too eagerly or Elva would never forgive me.

'Okay then,' I said in a couldn't-care-less sort of voice. 'Shall we be on our way?'

I didn't dare to look at Elva as I walked off

with Paul and I only hoped she would realise it hadn't been my fault.

When we reached the street I said to him, 'I can't think what you imagined might happen to me between here and the Nurses' Home.'

'Things do happen in ordinary safe-looking streets: murder, rape . . .'

'But not near the hospital!'

'What's that got to do with it?'

I didn't know and I relapsed into silence. Our footsteps made very little sound and we seemed to be wrapped around in a sort of cocoon which made me, at least, feel awkward and ill at ease. Ahead of us we could see the vast bulk of the hospital, its rows of lighted windows making it look like a giant liner with its portholes shining into the night. The Nurses' Home was a separate building at the right-hand side and the Medical School a much larger one at the other end.

Suddenly Paul said quietly, 'I'm afraid I used you as an excuse to make a getaway. You don't mind?'

'Not at all. Glad to have been of use,' I told him lightly. 'But I can't imagine why you wanted to escape. I thought you looked very much at home when I arrived out of the blue like that. I— I wished I hadn't come.'

Out of the corner of my eye I saw him turn his head and stare at me.

'What do you mean?'

'Exactly what I said. I felt I'd interrupted a cosy little scene for two. I wouldn't have stayed at all if I could have got away without making a ridiculous fuss.'

There was another short silence and then Paul said bleakly, 'That makes two of us.'

'You what?' The queer muffled feeling left me and I was suddenly gloriously alive. Then something made me add hastily, 'I don't understand.'

Paul didn't answer at once. We had reached the busy main road and he slipped his hand under my arm to guide me across. Automatically we turned towards the right. Eagerly I waited for him to tell me that Elva had practically bulldozed him into going to the flat for coffee.

But all he said was, 'Let's just leave it that I'm grateful to you for making my departure possible. And if you're looking for a reason, well—here's one which will do. I'm a bit short on sleep right now, having been up most of the last forty-eight hours. The prospect of an early night is very attractive.'

I felt unbelievably let down and I pointed out curtly that the Nurses' Home wasn't exactly on the direct route for him. 'Haven't you got a room somewhere up at the top of the hospital? You'd better make a beeline for it. I'm not likely to be murdered or raped now.'

'I'll finish the job properly, and that means seeing you to the door.'

The Nurses' Home had an imposing entrance with a stone canopy and two or three steps. Light streamed from it but just before we reached it there was a dark patch, much used by nurses to say goodnight to their boy friends. We seemed to be slowing down and my heart started beating in loud irregular thumps.

'I think this is far enough.' Paul stopped and I found he was holding my hands tightly in his.

I looked up at him expectantly. He had kissed me twice before and both times I hadn't been anticipating it. But tonight was different. As I stood there, so close to him that I could see the troubled look in his eyes in spite of the darkness, I knew that I *wanted* Paul to kiss me, wanted it with a desperate longing which frightened me.

But it didn't happen.

He was crushing my hands and I almost cried out in pain, but he didn't kiss me. He only stared at me with a strange intensity, muttered, 'Goodnight, Joanne—be seeing you some time,' and dropped my hands as though they'd burnt him. He went striding off at a tremendous speed and for a moment I just stood there, staring after him.

My emotions were in such a state of chaos that I had difficulty in pulling myself sufficiently together to enter the Nurses' Home. Up in my room I shut the door and locked it, and then sat down on my bed to try and talk some sense into myself.

Nothing could hide the face that I was bitterly disappointed because Paul hadn't kissed me. And yet—I was supposed to be in love with David, wasn't I? Then why did another man's kisses mean so much to me?

The answer was there, staring me in the face, but I wouldn't let myself see it. I pretended that David's moods were making me unhappy and I needed someone else to bolster up my self confidence and make me believe that I wasn't unattractive. This solution didn't show *me* in a very good light but anything was better than admitting the truth. I buried it in the deepest layer of my consciousness but couldn't forget it and when I was in bed I cried myself to sleep.

Elva wasn't on duty in the morning and when she arrived after lunch I managed to dodge her for quite a while. But inevitably the moment came when we met in the sluice where we'd both gone to dispose of bottles.

'I hope you got back all right last night?' she said sarcastically.

'Yes, thank you.'

'I can't think why you thought you needed an escort,' she went on. 'We've all walked alone along that street *millions* of times.'

I was stung by the injustice of her remark and lost some of the cool I'd been trying to maintain.

'I never suggested I needed an escort! Quite the contrary, in fact. And I don't suppose Paul thought I really required one either. It was just that he wanted to leave early to catch up on some sleep.'

'Did he tell you that?' she asked eagerly.

'Yes, of course. I wouldn't have known otherwise.'

My reply seemed to satisfy her and she changed the subject. 'I suppose you've noticed that Sister's moved Brian's bed—so David won't be annoyed by him any more?'

'That's good news—and it'll be even better when we hear he's being discharged,' I said fervently.

'You can say that again! But in the meantime we've got to put up with him being allowed up. Mr Greensmith said this morning he needn't stay in bed any longer. You'd better watch it, Jo.'

I had every intention of doing so. It seemed that Staff Nurse Leeming had carried out her threat of telling Sister and that was why she'd moved him out of David's room. But she didn't say anything to me about it and for that I was grateful. It meant she didn't necessarily accept Staff's version of the incident.

During the next few days I really did watch my step and managed to keep out of trouble. Then there came an evening when I was on late duty.

I quite liked staying on until ten o'clock. The

ward was quiet, with everybody in bed, but there was plenty to do what with bedtime medicines, treatments and hot drinks to give out.

On this particular evening I went round with the night junior, making sure patients were comfortable, collecting empty mugs and taking away unwanted pillows. Although we were busy, there was no sense of rush and we had time to stop and talk for a moment if that was what a patient wanted.

Naturally I lingered by David's bed but he had had his bedtime injection and was already sleepy. He didn't seem to care whether I was there or not and, after a swift look round, I gave him a quick kiss and moved on.

The night nurse was signalling to me urgently.

'Brian's bed is empty, Jo. What on earth can have happened to him?'

'Probably in the toilet.'

'No—there's nobody out there.'

'Did you look in the day room?' I asked. When she said hadn't got around to it I offered, without thinking, to do it myself.

The room was in darkness except for the glow from the TV set, which shouldn't have been on. At first I couldn't see anything and then spotted Brian's head above the back of an armchair.

'Time for bed.' I switched the set off. 'This room is out of bounds after nine o'clock.'

'So?' Brian made no attempt to move. 'I'm not

sleepy and I don't see any reason why I should go to bed just because Nursie tells me I'm supposed to.'

If I'd had any sense I would have switched on a light before I put the set off. The room was now almost completely dark, with the exception of the area near the open door, and Brian was sitting at the other end.

I said patiently, 'Come on—don't be tiresome. I'm off duty in a few minutes and I can't go until you're safely in bed.'

To my relief he stood up slowly and took a step forward. I was just turning to lead the way when his voice halted me.

'Nurse! I feel ever so queer—kinda faint——'

Afterwards, I couldn't imagine how I could have been such a fool as to fall for a corny line like that. But at the time my nurse's instincts were very much alert and I immediately went back and took his arm.

'Sit down again and put your head between your knees.' I steadied his tottering steps. 'Careful now—I don't want you collapsing on the floor.'

He subsided into a chair and I put my hand on his shoulder with a gentle pressure. The next moment I was seized in a grip of steel and I found myself sharing the chair with him, my body pressed hard against his and his mouth forcing my lips apart.

I couldn't move or cry out. I certainly

struggled but Brian's one arm was incredibly strong and I was utterly at his mercy, specially as he was pinning me against the side of the chair with his body as well.

How long it went on, I don't know, but it seemed an age and I suffered such revulsion as I'd never known before.

Then there was a sudden click and the room was flooded with light. Brian was startled and loosened his grip. Gasping, my cap hanging down the back of my neck, I scrambled to my feet.

Standing in the doorway the night staff nurse stared at me in incredulous disgust.

Never in all my life had I felt so humiliated. My face blazed with what must have looked like guilt. Frantically I scrabbled for my cap and tried to replace it. Beside me, Brian lounged comfortably in his chair, a grin of genuine amusement on his face.

'Go to the cloakroom, Nurse, and make yourself look presentable.' Staff Nurse Mason's voice was icy. 'Then come to the office. I shall be waiting for you.'

I went miserably to do as I was told. I was in trouble again and, as usual, it wasn't my fault. But as I tidied my hair and fixed my cap I felt uneasy. There was no denying I hadn't been as much on my guard as I should have been with a boy like Brian. I'd certainly had plenty of warning.

I could still feel the pressure of his mouth and I felt physically sick. But I didn't dare linger to wash my face. Staff had said she would be waiting.

I didn't know Staff Nurse Mason very well. She was married and a part-timer, but I suspected she was one of the old school like Leeming and I soon found out that I was right.

She was writing something when I arrived and she kept me waiting while she finished a sentence. Then she looked up, and it seemed to me that her eyes were the coldest I'd ever seen.

'Well, Nurse Marshall? What have you got to say for yourself?'

I blurted out the full story, freely admitting that I'd been an idiot to believe Brian. 'But I didn't want him to fall and hurt his arm and—and that was all I thought of.' I faltered under her steely gaze.

Her eyebrows rose. 'But what were you doing in the day room anyway? Did you go there to meet him?'

'No, I didn't! I only went to look for Brian and to tell him he must come to bed.'

She subjected me to a long stare and I could see she didn't know whether to believe me or not.

'You realise this is a very serious matter, Nurse,' she said at last.

'Yes, Staff.' I moistened my lips nervously.

'It's not for me to judge whether you're telling

the truth or not. I shall, of course, report the incident to your Sister in the morning.' She shook her head disapprovingly and dismissed me.

I went off duty feeling terribly depressed. Even a nice Sister like ours would sit up and take notice if *another* staff nurse reported me for bad behaviour with Brian.

Now, more than ever, I needed Paul's shoulder to cry on. But I had a horrible feeling that he'd withdrawn the offer.

CHAPTER NINE

As soon as Sister came on duty in the morning the Medway nurses realised she was in one of her rare bad moods. Her husband was an invalid but she hardly ever referred to him. It was only occasionally, when things weren't going too well at home, that she took it out on the nurses.

We all liked her so much we usually made allowances, but on that particular morning I wasn't in a good mood either.

She beckoned to me at the end of the report. 'I want to speak to you, Nurse Marshall. Come with me now.'

In the office I was told to sit down. I carefully folded back the corners of my apron and sat neatly, with feet tucked under, but I had to clasp my hands tightly together so she shouldn't see they were trembling.

'I'm very concerned about you, Nurse.' She looked at me keenly, her eyes troubled. 'Your work on the whole is good and I can depend on you to carry out instructions and not forget things. But your behaviour with the male patients is another matter. Three times I have received bad reports about you.'

'*Three* times, Sister?' I was indignant and didn't try to hide it.

'That is what I said. The first was perhaps excusable. I'm talking about the night when David Logan was brought in and you pretended to be the special nurse sent by the Night Superintendent. This was a serious offence but I made allowances for your state of mind as he was apparently your boy friend at the time.'

'He still is.'

'Really?' She was obviously finding it difficult to believe. 'Then why are you encouraging Brian's attentions? That seems to be both unkind and most unwise.'

I burst out passionately, 'I've *never* encouraged him, Sister! He's bored and he amuses himself by trying to get a rise out of me. As for last night, I explained to Staff exactly what happened and it's not my fault she didn't believe me.'

'She told me what you said.' Sister paused, frowning. 'I must say I think you were quite extraordinarily naïve to fall into such a trap—if you really did fall into it.'

My heart sank right down into my sensible low-heeled shoes. I'd never thought Sister Halliday would doubt my word.

'I *did* fall into it, daft as it seems.' My voice shook with the strength of my feeling. 'I—I hate Brian and nothing on earth would have induced me to let him kiss me if I'd realised it was going to happen.'

Sister looked shocked. 'A nurse should never *no matter what happens* allow herself to indulge in hatred for a patient! Sick people are not normal and every possible allowance must be made for them.'

I was silent, unhappily aware that I'd said the wrong thing.

'I think you've told me the truth,' Sister said after another pause, 'but I must admit that I'm not at all easy in my mind about you. No other nurse has had any trouble with Brian.'

'He made a dead set at me. He—he likes red hair.'

'I see.' I thought she repressed a smile but I wasn't sure. 'Well, Nurse Marshall, I shall have to consider what is to be done about you. Let me see, you've been on Medway for some weeks. When are you due to move?'

'In about a month's time, Sister.'

'H'm—well, in the meantime I'll discuss your case with a Senior Nursing Officer and perhaps your move can be speeded up. I don't know where you are going next but I can't help thinking a female ward would be a good idea. It seems to me you are not yet sufficiently mature for this ward. It's disappointing, of course, but there would be no point in my not being quite frank with you.'

She gave me an abrupt little nod of dismissal and I shot to my feet and out of the room.

As I returned to the ward I was burning with indignation. It wasn't fair! I'd been daft not to tell her about Brian right at the beginning but that wasn't a crime. The only thing I'd really done wrong was to pretend to be the special nurse and Sister had been very understanding on that occasion.

The nurses were busy getting the ward ready for the rounds of the various consultants who had patients in Medway. I joined in the activity but my mind was still occupied with my grievance, with the result that I dumped on David's locker a vase of flowers belonging to another patient.

He said languidly. 'Those aren't mine.'

'What?' I halted abruptly. 'Oh—sorry! I wasn't concentrating.' I took away the irises and sub-stituted some rosebuds which his mother had brought from their garden in London.

'Isn't it supposed to be rather dangerous for a nurse not to concentrate on what she's doing?' David enquired.

'Probably,' I snapped.

He raised his tufty eyebrows. 'What's the matter with you, then?'

'Sister's had me on the carpet because of Brian—and none of it was my fault.' I poured it all out, not forgetting the end bit about being moved to another ward in disgrace.

David listened with surprising patience. 'You've certainly had a raw deal, Jo, but not to worry. It'll all die down.'

'Only on the surface. Sister is bound to put it in my report when I leave Medway.'

'They won't hold it against you for ever.' He looked at me thoughtfully, hesitated and then seemed to make up his mind. 'Speaking personally, I wouldn't be all that sorry if you worked somewhere else.'

'You wouldn't?' I was outraged.

'Don't get me wrong. All I meant was that it isn't the happiest situation, being nursed by one's girl friend. I shouldn't think anything is more likely to kill romance stone dead.'

'I never thought of it like that——'

'Because you never looked at it from my point of view, only your own.'

It seemed to be my day for collecting brickbats but I accepted this one with unusual meekness. I'd seen quite a lot of romance in the situation and rather fancied myself in the role of ministering angel to David—in the beginning anyway. It had simply never occurred to me that he would have preferred to be nursed by strangers.

'I see what you mean,' I said thoughtfully.

He was thinking deeply and I felt there was more to come. When he began to speak again he avoided my eyes and stared down at the newspaper open on his bed table.

'I've got a rotten sort of future lined up for me at the moment, Jo. If you want to make a clean break when you go to another ward, I shall understand.'

I was so touched that tears rose to my eyes and I blinked furiously. I felt closer to David at that moment than I'd done for a long time.

'You mustn't talk like that,' I said impulsively. 'Of course I don't want to make a break. I'd never forgive myself——'

'Do you imagine I want you to stay with me out of pity?' David exploded.

'No, of course not.' Once more I'd said the wrong thing. 'Pity doesn't come into it—at least, not in the way you meant.' I pushed back a lock of hair and unsettled my cap. 'Oh dear—now I shall have to go and tidy myself. See you later, love!'

I managed to keep out of trouble for the rest of that day but I didn't have any more conversation with David. Not that it mattered. There was nothing more to be said.

I had a free weekend coming up in a week's time and began to look forward to it even more than usual. If I hadn't heard anything about being moved by then, I could surely conclude that the powers-that-be had decided to forgive me or—which would be more satisfactory— accept my version of the affair.

'What are you going to do with your weekend?' Elva asked. 'Something interesting?'

I shook my head. 'I shall go home, of course, and lie in bed all the mornings reading. With a bit of luck, somebody will bring me breakfast.' Seeing her amazement, I added defiantly, 'I know it sounds dull but I shall enjoy it. Anything to get away from this dump for a little while.'

'What's become of all your enthusiasm for your work?' she demanded curiously.

'I just happen to be a bit cheesed off, that's all.'

'Because of David, I suppose. He doesn't seem to be progressing at all.'

It wasn't just because of David. It was much more complicated than that but I didn't tell Elva.

Instead, I added with forced cheerfulness, 'At least I don't have any trouble with Brian now. I think Sister had a word with him.'

'He'll probably be discharged before you get back.'

I hadn't told her anything about the incident in the day room. I couldn't bear to talk about it. And she didn't know, either, about the trouble I was in with the authorities.

Just as I was beginning to hope I might hear no more about that, Sister called me into the office.

'Certain difficulties have arisen in the matter of your going to another ward, Nurse. As you must realise, it's not possible to move one nurse without involving others. However, I may have news for you soon.' She gave me rather a sad smile. 'I didn't want you to start imagining it had all been forgotten.'

She was in her normal mood this morning and I could see she was distressed because one of her nurses hadn't measured up to the standard required of her.

I said automatically, 'Thank you, Sister.'

'Perhaps after your weekend off, we shall be able to settle something. In the meantime, try and have a good rest. You've been looking rather overtired lately.'

Friday came at last and I finished at five o'clock. I was going to spend two nights and days at home, and return to the Nurses' Home on Sunday evening, ready for work on Monday morning early.

I packed a small case and carried it down to the bus stop. As I stood there waiting I was sharply reminded of the time when Paul picked me up and we went to Barhaven. It had been raining then, off and on, but this evening it was fine and warm. How absolutely wonderful it would be if he appeared again with a similar invitation!

I wouldn't be able to accept, of course, because Mum was expecting me for a meal but it would be nice just to have it happen.

It didn't happen. The bus came along, late as usual, and I got on and rode to my normal getting-off place in Strawton High Street. At home they seemed pleased to see me and I had a lazy enjoyable evening. My sister grudgingly promised to bring me breakfast in the morning.

I was lying in that delicious state which is neither sleeping nor waking when I was suddenly conscious that my bedroom door had opened. A shaft of sunlight from the landing poured into my room and I vaguely registered that Sue was standing there.

'Breakfast already?' I opened my eyes wider and peered at the clock. 'It's only half-past nine!'

'I haven't even started to get it. You're wanted on the phone.'

'What? Who on earth——?' I struggled into a sitting position.

'I don't know who it is. A man with rather a nice voice. Does that mean anything to you?'

Nothing meant anything except that I had to get out of bed and stagger downstairs. Barefooted, not bothering to put my dressing-gown on, I followed my sister out of the room and groped for the banisters. At that stage I was too dopey to be curious but when I reached the hall I suddenly woke up.

I simply couldn't imagine who it could be. For some time now David had been the only man in my life and I didn't think he'd be ringing.

I picked up the receiver and said a rather husky 'Hello!' into it, and immediately someone exclaimed, 'Joanne?' in a very doubtful sort of voice.

Only one person called me by my full name and my heart-beats suddenly doubled their rate. I said breathlessly, 'Yes—it's me. How—how on earth did you get hold of my home number?'

'I've just wasted ten minutes ringing up all the Marshalls in the Strawton area, and then when you came on the line you didn't sound like yourself and I wondered if I was wrong again. Listen, Joanne——' Paul's voice became more urgent. 'I've only got a minute left and I wanted to ask if you were doing anything tomorrow because the weather seems set fair and the tides are right for walking out to the island at Barhaven.'

I gasped and thought I must be dreaming. And then I felt sure that, although I was by now wide awake, Paul couldn't possibly mean what I'd at first imagined he did.

I said quickly, 'Thanks for telling me. I—I'll try and fix up a visit to Barhaven.'

Over the wires I could sense that he was taken aback and I knew I hadn't said what he was expecting to hear. As I puzzled over it his voice came again.

'I don't think you understood, Joanne. I was suggesting we might go together, since we're both a bit dotty about islands . . .'

I'd been right at the beginning! I was so excited I could hardly speak coherently.

'I'd love it, Paul! I'm absolutely free tomorrow—but what about you?'

'Would I have invited you if I'd been working?' I didn't blame him for being sarcastic. 'I guess you aren't really properly awake yet. It's my day off and I'm free until I go on call at ten o'clock. That will give us bags of time.'

He arranged to call for me around ten-thirty and I replaced the receiver in a daze of happiness.

'New boy friend?' My sister asked when I casually told her of the arrangements for Sunday.

'Of course not. Just—just someone I happen to know.' I escaped upstairs. 'How about bringing me my breakfast now?'

'You lazy so-and-so! Come and get it yourself if you want any. There's no need to go back to bed.'

But she relented and brought me toast and coffee, and I spent a heavenly morning doing absolutely nothing. I didn't even read. Somehow I didn't seem able to concentrate.

My family knew about David, of course, and I was aware that they were curious and not entirely approving when I got ready to go to Barhaven with Paul. I would have liked to prepare a picnic but I thought it better not to ask my mother if she had anything suitable.

I was listening for a car before half-past ten and as soon as Paul drew up I hurried out of the house and down the garden path. Maybe I appeared terribly over-eager but I didn't care. It seemed much more important that he shouldn't have to be introduced to anybody.

He was wearing jeans and I was glad I'd put mine on. Both of us had brought thick sweaters and anoraks in case the weather changed, and Paul said he'd also got some food so it was a good thing I hadn't bothered my mother. With all this preparation the outing seemed much more like an expedition than an ordinary Sunday trip to the coast.

'What time is low tide?' I asked as we raced along the dual carriageway.

'About noon, but I've made enquiries and it seems the causeway is passable for an hour or more before and after low tide. That will give us more time to explore thoroughly. Did you bring your swimming things?'

I said I had but I wasn't making any promises about going in the water. 'It's still early in the summer and it won't have warmed up much.'

'Coward!' Paul mocked, turning his head and giving me a quick smile which turned my heart over.

I was so happy just sitting there beside him that I wouldn't have minded how long the drive lasted. He was in a marvellous mood, quite different from how he'd been the last time we had any conversation together and the odd way he'd behaved when he walked back with me.

Today everything was going to be perfect.

We found Barhaven much busier than on our

previous visit. The weather had brought people flocking over from Thorpevale. They were staring in the shops, walking along the prom, sitting on the beach, and a few were even bathing.

'I hope it's not going to be like Piccadilly Circus on the island,' Paul said in disgust.

'I don't think so. People are afraid of getting cut off and they don't much like walking along the causeway either. It's very wet and in parts rather hard to follow. We shall have to be careful.'

'Didn't you say something about it being marked by posts?'

'Yes, but they're far apart and I wouldn't be surprised if some are missing.'

We came to the end of the prom and stopped to reconnoitre. A wide expanse of wet sand stretched before us, with little streams of water cutting across it. A sort of rough road made of stones started off from the beach, looking very firm at the beginning but rapidly deteriorating.

'Nice timing,' Paul said. He jumped down on to the sand. 'Come on, Joanne. Let's start the great adventure.'

'Why do you always call me Joanne?' I asked curiously as I joined him. 'The first time we ever met I told you my friends always shortened it to Jo, and when you continued to say Joanne I thought you wanted to emphasize that we were *not* friends.'

There was a tiny pause and then Paul asked, 'Do you still think that?'

'I—don't know,' I said stupidly, and then hastily amended it. 'I suppose I take it for granted now. But you haven't answered my question.'

'Joanne is a pretty name and I like it. It seems a pity to shorten it; after all, Jo could just as easily stand for Josephine and that wouldn't suit you at all.'

The explanation pleased me and we walked on in a companionable silence. It was becoming necessary to concentrate as there were numerous pools of water and the sand was squelchy so that our footprints left holes behind us. The stones were getting fewer and we hadn't even reached the second post.

Suddenly I slipped on some seaweed and Paul grabbed me to stop me landing on my knees. He kept hold of my hand as we splashed on our way.

'The island doesn't seem to be getting any nearer,' I said, staring ahead at the low mound covered with stunted bushes and short grass.

Paul glanced back over his shoulder. 'But the shore is rapidly getting farther away.'

I looked back too and was suddenly swept by a frightening sense of isolation. We were in the middle of nowhere, and if I hadn't had Paul with me I would have been scared.

But he *was* with me, his hand was warmly

holding mine and the moment of fear disappeared. Besides, the island really was growing larger now and in another few minutes we would be there.

'Has this place got a name?' Paul asked abruptly as we jumped over one of the wandering streams and landed on firmer ground.

'I expect so but I can't remember what it is,' I told him, beginning to walk up the beach. 'Everybody local always calls it "The Island".'

I stopped to stare back the way we had come and, joining me, he slipped his arm through mine.

'We'll give it our own special name, Joanne. Perhaps we'll think of something appropriate while we're here.'

'We shan't have much time for christening ceremonies.' I laughed. 'We've got to explore, and eat our lunch and—perhaps bathe. That will certainly use up all the time available.'

'I suppose it will.' Paul sounded regretful. 'It's a pity we haven't got longer.'

CHAPTER TEN

THERE was no one on the island. On that perfect June day it seemed to Paul and me that it was wholly ours. As we followed a rough track inland, winding between gorse bushes, with nothing overhead except the blue arch of the sky and nothing around except the odd sea bird, I felt utterly happy.

'What a super place to build a little stone cottage and use it for holidays and weekends,' Paul said. 'Imagine sleeping here with the wash of the sea in your ears, and then waking early and going for a swim——'

'It sounds lovely but I expect it would be horribly cold and you wouldn't be allowed to build anyway. The island must belong to somebody.'

'You're spoiling my dream,' he complained.

'I was only trying to—to be sensible.'

'Then don't.' He stopped and looked down at me. 'We didn't come here to be sensible, Joanne. At least I didn't. When I'm being sensible I keep as far away from you as I can.'

My heart was thudding and I stammered as I tried to answer him. 'I—I don't understand what you m-mean.'

'Forget it. I guess I was just talking out of turn.' He began walking again, striding along much too fast. 'Do you think we've reached the middle of the island yet?'

'This must be it. It seems to be the highest point.' I looked over my shoulder at Barhaven and thought how gloriously far away it seemed. 'If we go down to the coast again, Paul, we shan't be able to see anything except water. We could easily be right out in the ocean.'

So we walked down a slight slope towards the beach which lay on the opposite side to the mainland, and it was exactly as I'd expected. Nothing but sea and rocks and the two of us.

There was a tiny cove, with a patch of sand—ideal for bathing.

'Let's have a quick dip,' Paul suggested, 'and then lunch.'

'It'll be quick all right.' I slipped one foot out of its sandal and felt the water. 'Icy!'

'Only because your foot is hot after walking. Are you one of those bathers who go in slowly inch by inch and suffer agonies? It's far better to get wet all over at once.'

'Don't be so superior!' I laughed from sheer happiness and began to take off my jeans.

I was wearing my bikini underneath them and Paul had his own swimming gear on as well. As my body emerged into the sunshine I was ashamed of its whiteness. Paul, being dark, was a much better colour. His skin was very clear and smooth, the hair lying sleekly, and there wasn't a spare ounce of flesh on him anywhere.

We'd only seen each other fully dressed before and for a moment an odd restraint descended on us. But we both shook it off without any difficulty and for the next fifteen minutes behaved like a couple of kids. We raced each other into the water, splashed, swam a little way and then floated, enjoying the hot sun. After that Paul ducked me and I came up spluttering and gasping and tried to duck him but couldn't manage it.

By that time the stinging exhilarating cold was getting a bit too much and we were glad to leave the water and lie on the warm sand to dry off.

'Did you enjoy it?' Paul asked, his voice sounding very close.

'It was heavenly! I feel ten years younger than I did on Friday.'

He raised himself on his elbow and stared down at me. 'You look quite different with your hair wet,' he observed in an interested tone.

'Better, I hope,' I said drowsily.

'I don't know.' He suddenly rolled away from me and his tone changed. 'How about some lunch? I'm starving.'

He'd brought ham and rolls and tomatoes, some fruit pies and even a bottle of wine, all of which came out of a small haversack. Still in our swimming things we ate hungrily and finished the bottle.

'How much longer have we got?' I asked as we tidied up the litter.

'Don't talk about time, Joanne!' His voice was suddenly so taut that I looked at him in surprise.

'I don't want to think about it but——'

'But you feel we ought to? How right you are.' He looked at his watch. 'Nearly another hour.'

'As much as that?' I was surprised and pleased. 'You're sure you haven't made a mistake?'

'Do you think I'm daft? It wasn't quite low tide when we crossed and that gives us a bit of margin. Plenty of time to lie in the sun for a while.'

I subsided again with a sigh of pleasure. Between half closed lids I stared up into the still cloudless sky, and thought that I had rarely known such perfect bliss. My eyes closed completely and I surrendered to the combined effects of cold water, hot sun, plenty of food and, of course, the wine.

Had I had more than my ration of two glasses? I wasn't sure and didn't care. Paul would have seen to it that I didn't drink too much, I reasoned sleepily.

It was my last thought for some time.

When I woke up I couldn't for a moment think where I was. There was something heavy—an arm?—lying across my body and another person lay so close that I felt deliciously warm and protected all down one side.

I was suddenly very wide awake. Paul must have dropped off too and was still asleep, his head against my shoulder. It was such heaven to have him there that I kept perfectly still, hardly daring to breathe.

But perhaps he wasn't as deeply unconscious as I had been. Whatever the reason, he stirred and must have sensed that I wasn't asleep any more. I felt him move but he didn't take his arm away; instead, he tightened it, pressing his hand against my bare back.

'Oh God, Joanne!' The words were almost a groan. 'I can't help it—I've just got to kiss you and—and I don't think I shall ever want to stop.'

I wanted it too and I surrendered eagerly. He kissed my lips, my neck and my breasts, fondling me with little murmured words of love, and I knew without either of us needing to say it that we both wanted much, much more than kisses.

Paul stopped at last and somehow got himself under control. We sat up and stared out across the sea, not touching each other.

'What are we going to do, Joanne? It's a devil of a difficult situation.'

'Just tell me you love me,' I begged. 'I must know for sure.'

'I love you,' he said solemnly and they seemed the most beautiful words I had ever heard. 'How do you feel about me?'

'I love you too. I've been trying not to but——'

'Do you think I haven't tried to put *you* out of my mind? But you wouldn't go; you were stuck there like—like a wasp in a jar of jam.'

I laughed shakily. 'That could have been better put!'

'I'm no good at pretty speeches.' He took my hand and held it tightly but didn't move any nearer. 'What *are* we going to do? You side-stepped the question just now but it's got to be answered.'

'About David, you mean?' An unwelcome thought struck me. 'There's Elva too.'

'She's not important.' Paul hesitated. 'I feel a bit of a heel saying it but we've got to be frank with each other. Elva made things—difficult. You know what I mean?'

I guessed he meant she'd been chasing him and I dismissed Elva from my mind, though not without a moment of regret.

'We must tell David as soon as possible,' I decided. 'It's not fair to keep it a secret. Besides, I can't go on pretending.'

Paul hesitated. 'Have you any idea how he would take news of that sort? He's very far from fit, you know.'

The question brought me up sharply. I thought for a few seconds before replying.

'We haven't been getting on at all well lately. But I can't be sure whether it's due to his being ill or whether he's really got fed up with me. He

147

actually said he was glad when I told him I might be moved to another ward.'

Paul was instantly alert. 'What's this then? I didn't know you were due for a move.'

And so I had to tell him about Brian and he scolded me for keeping it to myself and not complaining to Sister. I accepted it meekly because I knew he was right, and then brought the conversation back to David.

'I honestly don't think he'll be heartbroken——'

'You can't be sure with a bloke in his condition.' Paul seemed very worried. 'If you can possibly manage it, Joanne, I think you'd better wait a little while. Things have got to change one way or the other before long. I mean, he can't go on as he is now.'

I turned my head to look at him. 'What's that supposed to mean? I thought Mr Greensmith had done all he could and he was just waiting for the leg to heal, and that David was almost certainly going to be a cripple.'

'Well, yes—that's all true. But——' Suddenly Paul broke off and leapt to his feet, startling me. '*Hell*, Joanne—the time! Get your clothes on—quick!'

When I glanced at my own watch I was horrified. We'd never make it . . . I began to drag my jeans on with clumsy fingers and then my tee shirt and the sweater, because I had started feeling cold. My sandals were full of sand and the strap wouldn't do up. Then Paul was ready before I was.

'Do *hurry*!' he begged me. 'Perhaps if we run all the way to the other beach——'

But although we kidded ourselves I think we both knew there wasn't much hope. As I pounded along behind him, an idiotic jingle kept going through my head: 'Time and tide wait for no man.' It was on a piece of Devonshire pottery Mum kept on the sideboard and any minute now we were going to discover how terribly true it was.

We came at last to the beginning of the causeway and with a tremendous surge of relief I saw it was quite dry.

'We've made it after all!'

I turned excitedly to Paul and immediately noticed he wasn't sharing my elation. He shook his head and pointed towards the mainland. Between us and the distant shore there was a rippling expanse of water, still shallow, no doubt, but increasing steadily in width.

'Perhaps, if we're quick, we could wade across?' I suggested.

'It would be much too dangerous. The tide's coming in like a mill race and we'd be swept away. No point in both of us getting drowned.'

I couldn't have agreed more. Since the discovery that Paul loved me, life had become doubly precious.

'But what are we going to *do*? How long

before we can get over the causeway in safety?

Paul sat down on a rock and rested his elbows on his knees. I could see he was desperately worried and I remembered he had to be at the hospital by ten o'clock.

'It was low tide around noon—that means it won't be low again until after midnight. We shan't be able to walk over much before eleven.' He looked up at me. 'Where were you expecting to sleep tonight, Joanne?'

'At the Nurses' Home but it doesn't matter about me. You're the one we've got to worry about. I suppose someone will stand in for you if you don't turn up?'

'The other registrar's been on duty all the weekend but I suppose he'll remain on call *if* he knows I'm not there. But he may take it for granted I'm around and that could mean nobody's available.'

'The housemen——'

'They can't cope with everything. In a real emergency they'd expect to be able to bring in a registrar.'

I knelt down on the sand beside him and leaned against his shoulder. 'I think you're being unnecessarily pessimistic, Paul. You won't be more than about two hours late and it would be really bad luck if something blew up during that time.'

'These things happen——'

'But they don't *have* to happen.'

I was beginning to view the situation rather differently. To be marooned on an island with Paul for hours and hours wasn't far short of my idea of heaven.

'It's lucky it's not cold,' I went on in a determinedly cheerful tone. 'I just wish we hadn't eaten up all the food.'

That made him smile. 'I believe there's a bar of chocolate in the haversack but nothing else. You'd better have it, since your need seems to be greater than mine.'

'We'll share it—one piece each every hour. That will help the time to pass.' I jumped to my feet. 'But don't let's stay here staring at the causeway. It was much nicer on the other side of the island.'

Paul stood up slowly and, it seemed to me, reluctantly.

'I've just thought of something,' he said. 'We might be able to attract attention by waving to a boat——'

'There aren't any boats.' I gazed at the empty sea.

'Fishermen often don't come out until the evening. We must keep a sharp lookout later on.' He glanced disapprovingly at our clothing. 'What a pity neither of us is wearing anything red.'

'I've got a red scarf in my pocket.' I produced

it and waved it aloft. 'It's my sister's actually—I never wear red because of my hair—and she left it in the pocket when she borrowed the anorak some time.'

'It isn't big enough to be seen more than a few yards, particularly if it was getting dark.' Paul thrust his hands into his pockets and hunched his shoulders. 'I'm afraid there isn't much hope we shall be rescued so——'

'So we'll just have to make the best of it.' I couldn't help my voice sounding a little despondent. 'I'm sorry you're going to hate it so much.'

'Hate it?' Paul seized me by the arms and swung me round to face him. 'You darling stupid girl, Joanne—can't you see I'm afraid of enjoying it too much? Right now I can't think how I'm going to be able to spend all this time with you without making love. I want it so much——'

'I want it too,' I whispered. 'But——'

'But we've got to avoid it somehow. If David was healthy, instead of in hospital and going through hell, then you'd just tell him you didn't want to be his girl friend any more and that would be that——'

'I thought we agreed I was to tell him?' I interrupted.

'Yes, but I asked you to wait a little longer. Remember?' I nodded and Paul went on, 'That being the case, I think we ought to do our best to behave ourselves—or am I being a damn fool not to make the most of my chances?'

I knew he was right. I was going to feel guilty enough the next time I saw David without the secret knowledge that I'd betrayed him with someone else.

'I think perhaps I might not love you quite so much if—if you really did take advantage of the situation,' I admitted.

'Good!' He kissed me fervently. 'And now let's come down off the heights of heroic self-discipline and decide how we're going to pass the time.'

It seemed to me that it passed quite quickly, but perhaps that was only because I was with Paul. At first we talked a lot, telling each other all about our families, our childhood and schooldays. We learnt a tremendous amount about each other during those hours of isolation, more than we would have found out during months of ordinary life.

I discovered that Paul adored all kinds of seafood whereas I'm not at all fond of fish.

'I hope you'll feed me on fish sometimes when we're married,' he said. 'I wouldn't like to give it up completely, even for you, love.'

'When we're married——' I began dreamily and then broke off to remind him he hadn't asked me yet.

'I would like us to get married, Joanne,' Paul told me seriously, holding my hands very tightly. 'I don't want us just to live together like so many couples do. I've nothing against it in a way—I just feel it's not for me. I want to see you in bridal white, coming down the aisle towards me.' He stopped and laughed in an embarrassed sort of way. 'I expect you think that's ridiculously old-fashioned?'

I thought it was marvellously romantic and I said so promptly. 'I think on the whole girls prefer marriage but they're afraid to say so in case the fellas take fright.'

'I shan't take fright,' he assured me. 'I couldn't be happy if you were free to go off and leave me any time you chose.'

After that we didn't talk for quite a while so that when we looked round again it was nearly dark and Paul said he thought we should go and watch for boats.

'If only we could hitch a ride back, I might not be late after all.' He jumped up and pulled me to my feet in the sandy hollow where we had been keeping each other warm.

We did see a few fishermen in the failing light but they were too far away to notice our frantic waves. We had another piece of chocolate each and resigned ourselves to waiting until the cause-way was passable.

That last hour or so really did seem long. Paul was on edge and I knew he was thinking about the hospital instead of me. I didn't mind; if I was going to marry a doctor I would have to get used to that.

When we at last started out along the causeway I was terrified. We went very slowly, testing each step because it would have been so easy to stray into the water and there was little to guide us. The posts which were supposed to mark the route were invisible in the darkness.

It seemed an age before the track became firmer and began to rise and I knew we were almost at the end. Thankful as I was to reach safety, I was also conscious of an odd feeling of regret. Just for a moment I looked back at the dark shape of the island.

Some people might think it a dreadfully dull little place but I knew it would be for ever enshrined in my memory as the spot where I discovered Paul loved me. There were difficulties ahead for us both, but somehow we would surmount them and truly belong to each other.

'Come on,' Paul said. 'Let's run.'

He set off at a great pace and we were soon at the car. Once clear of Barhaven we tore along the dual carriageway but although I understood his fever of impatience, I didn't share it. There were problems of my own which I would have to face when we reached Thorpevale.

'I'll drop you off at the Nurses' Home,' Paul told me, 'and then rush along to the switchboard to tell the operator I'm here.'

'It won't be any good.'

'What won't?'

'Leaving me at the Nurses' Home. The door will be locked for the night.'

'Hell! That was all it needed. What are you going to do then? You don't want me to turn round and drive you home?'

I put his mind at rest on that. 'There's no need to disturb my parents. I'll go along to the flat and throw myself on their mercy.'

'Good idea. They don't keep early hours there,' Paul agreed and I couldn't help a tiny feeling of reproach because he was so obviously glad I wasn't going to be a burden to him.

I knew it was unreasonable and I pushed it down quickly. I even made amends by saying I could walk from the hospital car park, which would get him on duty a few minutes earlier.

'You'll do nothing of the sort at this time of night.' Paul turned away from the hospital and then suddenly jammed on the brake so that I was flung forward and nearly bumped my head. 'Oh God—did you see what I saw?'

'No—what?' I stared about me.

'The boss's car. That means he's been called out and he'll certainly take a dim view if neither of his registrars was available. There'll be the devil to pay tomorrow.'

'Oh, Paul—I'm so sorry,' I said wretchedly.

He kissed me quickly. 'It wasn't your fault. And now let's get you to the flat as fast as possible.'

CHAPTER ELEVEN

I HAD a stroke of luck when I got to the flat. Tony was just coming out and Lorna said at once that I could stay the night.

'I'm afraid there isn't a bed, Jo. You'll have to make do with the settee.'

I said I didn't mind and was grateful she'd accepted my arrival without question. She knew I'd been staying at home and I suppose she thought I'd cut it too fine or—more likely—she didn't bother herself about it at all.

Perhaps it was all that sea air; whatever the reason I slept very well. I awoke with a delicious feeling of happiness but as soon as I opened my eyes it vanished.

Elva was standing there in her dressing-gown, staring down at me in amazement.

'What on earth are you doing here, Jo? Who let you in?'

'Lorna. You don't mind, do you? I got back too late from my free weekend to get in at the Nurses' Home.' I sat up and looked at her defiantly.

'Sounds like very bad management to me. You were staying at home, weren't you? Why didn't you leave in good time?'

I shrugged. 'I—er—thought I had. Are you on early duty? If so, we'd better both get cracking.'

I could see she wasn't satisfied with my feeble explanation but didn't let it bother me. I jumped up and asked her to tell me when the bathroom was vacant but she didn't answer. She was still standing there with a most peculiar expression on her face.

'Jo——' She stopped abruptly.

Her tone had been so full of meaning that I was suddenly scared.

'Are you trying to tell me something?' I demanded.

Elva sat down on a chair and twisted her hands together. It came to me that she was feeling genuinely distressed.

'Go on,' I urged. 'I can see you've got news of some sort——'

'I'm afraid it's bad news, Jo. While you were enjoying yourself on your free weekend David got much worse. His temperature rocketed and Mr Greensmith decided he'd have to amputate the leg. The operation's today. I—I thought I'd better tell you before you went on duty.'

I stared at her aghast and I could literally feel myself going white. Poor, poor David—what a terrible thing to happen. I felt overwhelmed with shame as I remembered how happy I'd been yesterday.

'How—how did he take it?' I asked at last.

'Very well, but they'd got him so doped that maybe it didn't really sink in. He'd forgotten you were off duty and asked where you were.' She stood up and gave me a look of pity tinged with slight bitchiness. 'You'd better be practising what you're going to say to him. It won't be easy.'

'You're telling me!' I sighed and ran my fingers through my hair. 'I reckon I'd better play it by ear. Oh dear—I can hardly take it in yet. Somehow I never thought of this.'

'I got the impression it had been on the cards for quite a while,' Elva said over her shoulder as she went into the kitchen. 'Mr Greensmith put it off as long as possible, of course, because he wanted to save the leg.'

As I struggled out of the sleeping bag Lorna had lent me I suddenly thought of something. Paul had advised me to wait for a short time before telling David about us. Was this what was in his mind?

A cold sick feeling of dread overwhelmed me in addition to the horror I was already feeling because of David. How would I ever be able to tell him now that this awful thing had happened?

Time was flying. I shook off the strange inertia which had seized me and began to dress. After a quick drink of much needed coffee, I raced off to the hospital to get into uniform.

The ward was busy and the early morning rush was my salvation. I'd taken a peep at David when

I went in but he appeared to be still asleep. It wasn't until things calmed down a bit that I had any conversation with him.

Because of the operation he was to have no breakfast and the night nurses had left him as he was, lying down. I went right up to the bed and put my hand on his where it lay outside the bed-clothes. His lids lifted slowly and he looked into my face with eyes glazed by sedatives.

'Jo—I thought you were never coming——'

'I had two days off duty.'

'You know, I suppose?'

'Yes.' I took his hand in both mine but it felt limp and unresponsive. 'Oh, David—David darling—I can't tell you how sorry I am.'

'It's hellish luck,' he murmured after a pause. 'But I suppose I've got to come to terms with it.'

I tried to think of something comforting. 'It may not be as bad as you think. People with artificial legs seem able to do almost everything. Could be it'll be better than being a cripple.'

'That's what I keep telling myself. There was that guy who was so famous during the war. Bader, wasn't it? I saw the film ages ago. There wasn't much he couldn't do.'

'You'll be the same. Going to the disco again and—and everything.'

'Not playing rugger,' he said bitterly.

'Well—no. But you'd have given that up soon

anyway. You wouldn't have had time for rugger after you qualified.'

David didn't answer and we remained silent for a moment, his hand still in mine. I was just beginning to speak again when I was conscious that someone had come up behind me and had picked up the chart.

It was Paul.

As I stood there, holding David's hand and with every fibre of my being aware of Paul's nearness, I felt so confused and unhappy that for a moment nothing seemed real—neither yesterday and those magical hours on the island, nor the terrible ordeal which David must face in a short time. Not even my own emotions.

With an effort I pulled myself together. 'I must go, love.' I gave his hand a quick squeeze. 'See you later.'

Without a glance at Paul, who was certainly taking no notice of me, I walked away.

We served breakfast and then began to clear it away and tidy the ward. Lucy hadn't eaten much of hers, which was unusual as she had a good appetite for such a fragile-looking little person.

'What's up with you then?' I asked her, noticing her drooping mouth.

'I keep thinking about that poor boy——'

'Who? D'you mean David?'

'Yes, of course. We all know about the amputation. It does seem so awful——.' She broke off and swallowed. 'Why couldn't Mr Greensmith get it to mend properly?'

I didn't want to talk about it but I knew she'd developed a sentimental fondness for David recently and I felt I ought to try and explain.

'It wasn't just that the bone was shattered. Most of the nerves and blood vessels were damaged too. Mr Greensmith wouldn't have taken such a drastic step if he hadn't known gangrene was setting in.'

'Gangrene!' Her little round face was screwed into a grimace of disgust. 'I don't know *exactly* what that is and I don't want to, so please don't give me any details.'

'I wasn't going to.' I began stacking her dishes. 'I shouldn't be talking to you at all about David. We aren't supposed to discuss one patient with another.'

'I don't see why not.' She changed the subject. 'How's that patient who woke us all up in the night? Not that it was her fault, poor thing,' she added hastily. 'She couldn't help being so badly smashed up in a car accident.'

'I've been off duty all the weekend and haven't really caught up yet.' I forced a smile. 'Looks like you know more about the ward than I do, Lucy!'

The patient she'd referred to, I soon discovered, was in our smallest room, one containing only three beds. She'd been brought in late the previous evening in such a bad condition that she'd had to be treated for severe shock and loss of blood before much could be done about her injuries. Just like David, in fact.

I didn't want to think about him and I flung myself into work with an intense nervous energy which made me feel I never wanted to stop. From a distance I saw him being taken off to the theatre and soon after that it was time for my coffee break.

Usually I enjoyed the brief rest and made the most of it but this time I drank my coffee quickly and went out into the grounds. I felt restless and uneasy and I thought a few minutes brisk walk might help.

I was charging through the narrow passage which led to the tennis courts when I saw someone coming towards me—a man in a white coat. And when I saw it was Paul I wanted to turn and run.

If we'd planned a meeting we couldn't have managed it more neatly but I didn't want to see him just then. Too much lay between us, holding us apart. There was a lot of sorting out to be done and I didn't feel equal to it.

As soon as we met it struck me that he looked very strained too but we both made an effort to speak naturally.

'How come you're wandering around the grounds in the middle of the morning?' I said carelessly.

163

'I might say the same about you.'

I explained about my coffee break and the need for fresh air, adding with a horrible forced lightness, 'It's your turn now.'

'I'm out of a job,' Paul said.

My heart turned over as I took him entirely literally. 'Oh, Paul—no! Did Mr Greensmith find out you were late? He surely wouldn't give you the sack just for that!'

'Just a minute, Joanne!' He gave me a little shake. 'I didn't mean anything as terrible as you're apparently imagining. But it's quite bad enough. He as good as told me he didn't want to see my face in the theatre this morning.'

'So he did find out——'

'Yes. It was hellish bad luck. Tim—the other registrar—assumed, without checking, that I was back and went off home, only he didn't go home actually but to a very late party. Then there was a bad crash—you've got the victim in Medway—and the housemen panicked when the Casualty Officer sent the patient up to the ward. They couldn't get hold of a registrar and one of them rang up the boss. As you can guess, he wasn't at all pleased.'

I listened in an appalled silence, tried to find something sympathetic to say and failed utterly. It seemed to me that everything was going wrong because Paul and I loved each other.

'At least I shan't have to assist at David's operation,' he finished bleakly.

'Did you know it was likely to happen? The amputation, I mean.'

'It certainly seemed probable but——'

I was suddenly in a furious temper. 'Then why on earth didn't you tell me? I think it was terrible of you to let me think David might get better——'

Paul interrupted in his turn. 'How could I possibly say anything of the sort? It's not my job to go around telling other people Mr Greensmith's private thoughts about a patient.'

'I'm not "other people"—I'm David's girl friend, or at least I'm supposed to be.' I faced him stormily.

'And in any case, you knew perfectly well David would never get better in the fullest sense of the expression. He was bound to be crippled. To my mind, he'll be better off with an artificial limb.'

It was what I had said myself to David only a little while ago but I resented hearing it from Paul.

'I suppose to you he's just a patient,' I said bitterly, 'but to me he's a person—someone who matters.'

There was a horrible silence. I stood miserably staring at the ground, quite unable to meet Paul's eyes. I couldn't understand why I felt so angry with him. Every trace of the marvellous relationship we'd had yesterday seemed to have vanished.

Had he really said he wanted to marry me? If so, he must be regretting it now.

I wasn't at all sure I wanted to marry *him*. This cold-eyed man who faced me now wasn't the Paul I'd learnt to love. He was much more like the one I'd first met at Lorna's party.

'I must go.' I turned away abruptly. 'I daren't risk being late back.'

Luckily there was plenty to do. Our new patient was in a bad way and needed constant watching. Her husband sat by her side in a sort of stupor, but every now and then he demanded angrily why somebody didn't 'do something' about his wife.

'She's got multiple fractures—why don't they set them? She can't go on like this.'

Sister explained gently that we were building up her strength with the drip and giving her a chance to get over the shock of the accident.

'How long are you going to leave her then?' he asked.

'I couldn't say but perhaps until this evening.'

About five o'clock Paul came in to tell the husband that his wife would shortly be fetched. I was desperate for news of David and I managed to snatch a word with him before he left the ward.

'He's still in the recovery room.' His eyes met

mine briefly. 'I'm sure you'll be glad to know he stood the operation very well, but an amputation is a terrible shock to the whole system—nerves, heart, everything. I think he'll be kept under observation until tomorrow.'

'Thank you.' I was painfully polite. 'Have you—er—been reinstated in the theatre?'

'Apparently. I'm to help with your patient.' He smiled faintly. 'We're so darned busy that every pair of hands is needed.'

I felt a little more cheerful after that. Mr Greensmith had apparently forgiven Paul and David was going to be all right. But I still didn't dare to think about the future.

Other people had apparently been giving some thought to it. Just as I was going off duty Sister called me.

'One moment, Nurse Marshall.' She ushered me into the office. 'Your move has been arranged at last and you are to start on Trent next Sunday. It's a women's medical ward and I'm sure it will suit you well.'

Automatically I said, 'I hope so, Sister, thank you.'

She gave me a sharp look. 'You're very pale— are you feeling all right?'

I hastily explained that it had been a heavy day and I was tired.

Sister nodded. 'I think we've all found it trying, and I expect you've been worried about

David. Did you know he was doing all right?'

'Er—yes, somebody told me, thanks.'

'You'll be relieved not to have to nurse him, I should think.' She dismissed me with a wave of her hand. 'Try and get a good night's rest.'

There wasn't much hope of that. I lay awake for hours, trying to make some sense out of the situation in which I found myself and failing miserably. David's amputation seemed to have changed everything.

He was brought back to the ward during the morning and looked dreadful, almost worse than when he was first brought into the hospital. Luckily he was heavily sedated and made few demands on anyone.

It was two days before I had any conversation with him. As soon as I came on duty I could see he was much better. He was sitting up reading the newspaper but when he saw me he put it down and waved.

'Hi, Jo! It seems quite a while since I saw you.'

'You haven't been seeing anyone just lately.' I smiled with genuine pleasure. 'It's great to see you're feeling much more like yourself.'

'I don't know what myself is now—I'll have to get used to a new person.' He grimaced. 'It's a funny thing but I can't realise my leg isn't there. I mean, I can still feel it.'

'I believe that's usual after an amputation.'

'So they tell me. How are things with you, Jo?

Everything going okay?'

It was so long since he'd taken any interest in my welfare that I was really touched. For one wild delirious moment I wondered whether to tell him about Paul but I instantly dismissed the idea. It was much too soon after the operation.

Besides, I no longer felt certain that Paul wanted to go on with it.

'You're taking a long time to answer a simple question,' David complained. 'What's on your mind?'

'Only that I'm being moved to another ward at the end of the week.' I paused and then added diffidently, 'Maybe you'll be glad?'

The news had certainly caught his interest. He looked at me thoughtfully.

'Which would you rather have, Jo? Truth or pretence?'

'I certainly don't want you to pretend so it'd better be the truth. Actually, though, I don't think you need say anything because I remember you told me once you didn't like being nursed by me. I don't suppose you've changed your mind.'

'No.' The answer was prompt and definite. 'Since you want me to be frank, I *am* glad you're going.'

'Now we know where we stand,' I said lightly.

I had a feeling David was going to say something else but at that moment the icy voice of Staff Nurse Leeming cut into our conversation.

'No doubt you only come to the ward to hold conversations with the patients, Nurse Marshall, but I'm afraid I must remind you that a nurse does have other duties.'

The sarcastic old cow . . . I moved away from David's bed hastily and found a job to do at the other end of the ward. I kept out of her way for the rest of the day, and that meant I didn't talk to David any more.

My last day in Medway came. I felt sad and relieved both at the same time, an unhappy mixed-up state which seemed to be becoming normal with me.

I couldn't leave without saying goodbye to David, even though I intended to visit him as much as possible. Choosing my moment carefully I lingered by his bed after supper, when the ward was relaxing before the evening visitors arrived.

'So it's goodbye, Jo,' he said in such a serious tone that I was taken aback.

'Not really—I shall be coming to see you——' I began, only to find myself interrupted.

'You said the other day you didn't want me to pretend and I'd rather you didn't pretend either.' He held my gaze so that I couldn't look away. 'You know as well as I do that whatever there was between us died the night of the accident. We've been flogging it ever since, trying to get some life into it, but it's no good. Maybe it never would have been any good—who knows?

I'm damned if I do.'

'Oh, David——' I was close to tears. 'Are you—are you sure?'

'Course I'm sure.' He patted my hand in a fatherly way. 'Don't look so upset—you know you're not really. I wouldn't mind betting you've just heard the best news of your life.'

'I *am* upset.' I brushed my hand across my eyes and blinked rapidly. 'This isn't like an ordinary parting of the ways, with you in hospital and—and everything. I can't help feeling sad.'

'Only because you're a sentimental idiot,' David said severely. 'It's a good thing one of us has got a bit of sense—and that's my last word on the subject. Cheerio, love—enjoy your new ward!'

I rushed out of the room and disappeared into the cloakroom. As I mopped my eyes and then splashed them with cold water I couldn't think why I didn't feel happier.

Nothing now stood between Paul and me. I ought to be on top of the world.

CHAPTER TWELVE

TRENT was a very different ward from Medway. Large and old-fashioned, it had beds down both sides and half of them at least contained acute cases. The accident ward had, on the whole, been a cheerful place and at first I couldn't get used to the quietness of Trent.

The sister was youngish and I liked her at once. She made no reference to the reason why I'd been sent to her and immediately assumed I was a responsible second-year nurse capable of working on her own if necessary.

It was just what I needed and I flung myself into my new job, determined to do well in my career even if my private life seemed to have fallen apart.

For the first week I saw nothing of my old friends, and then one day I met Elva in the canteen where I was drinking a cup of tea.

'How's it going then?' She sat down at the same table and began eating a chocolate biscuit hungrily.

'Fine! I like nursing medical cases,' I said truthfully. 'Er—how's David?'

Her finely marked brows rose. 'I'm surprised

you don't know! As far as I can make out you haven't been to see him once since you left Medway.'

'So?' I tilted my chin and returned her gaze defiantly.

'For crying out loud!' Elva exploded. 'He's your boy friend, isn't he?'

'You're out of date, love. David himself suggested we'd come to the end, just before I left. I agreed with him and we parted friends.'

'And you believed him? Oh, Jo—how could you be so thick!' Her eyes were wide with surprise and deeply reproachful. 'Of course he didn't mean it—he was just being chivalrous. You can understand a guy not wanting to tie a girl down when he's lost a leg. It's only natural. But he didn't expect you to *believe* it.'

I stared back at her in dismay, badly shaken. I desperately wanted her to be wrong—I was very nearly sure she *was* wrong—and yet there was that underlying doubt.

'He certainly didn't sound like a man trying to kid his girl friend into thinking he didn't love her any more, and all the time hiding a broken heart. David just isn't the type for heroics.'

Elva looked stubborn. 'Perhaps you don't know him very well.'

'Of course I know him!' I put down my cup with a bang and stood up. 'But just to set your mind at rest I'll come along to Medway and visit him at the first opportunity. I'll be able to tell from the expression on his face whether he wants to see me or not.'

I was free in the afternoon the following day. Wearing my new summer dress I joined the crowd of visitors waiting outside Medway and went in with them. It seemed strange to enter the familiar ward as someone from the outside world, who didn't belong. I immediately glanced round, hoping I wouldn't meet any of the nurses— hoping, above all, that Paul wouldn't be there.

The curtains were drawn round the bed opposite David's, the one which Brian had occupied, but I scarcely noticed because I was so surprised to see David up and sitting in a wheeled chair.

'This is great!' I smiled at him radiantly, quite forgetting the purpose of my visit. 'Why did nobody tell me you'd been promoted?'

'Why didn't you come and see me and find out? It's been more than a week.' His voice was full of reproach and he took my hand and held it. 'I've missed you, Jo.'

'For heaven's sake—I thought you were longing to get rid of me!'

'Well, I was wrong, wasn't I? As soon as you'd gone I wished I hadn't been so definite. And then when you didn't come to visit me, I knew you'd taken me too seriously.'

My head was whirling and I leaned back against the edge of the bed. I couldn't fetch myself a chair because David was still holding my hand.

'I just don't understand you,' I said blankly. 'First you more or less tell me you never want to see me again—and now you're accusing me of neglecting you. None of it makes any sense.'

'It makes sense to me,' David told me. Suddenly he gave me a sharp look. 'Good God, Jo—you're not imagining I want to go back to how things used to be between us, do you? Is that why you're looking so shattered?' He burst out laughing. 'If you could see your appalled expression! It's not very flattering.'

'I can't help that——'

'No, of course, you can't.' He was still laughing. 'It's not as bad as you thought, love—I only want us to go on being ordinary friends. Do you reckon you can manage that?'

'I—I think I could.'

'Then give me a kiss to seal the bond and show there's no ill will.' He pulled me down to his level and kissed me enthusiastically.

It was at that exact moment that the curtains opposite parted and Paul came out. Our eyes met across the space between the two beds but the expression in his was beyond my understanding. I don't know what he saw in mine but I could feel my face turning pink with embarrassment.

If Elva had planned the whole thing to thrust a wedge between Paul and myself she couldn't have been more successful. I knew it wasn't her fault. She suspected there was something between us and wanted to make sure I stayed with David. I couldn't possibly hold her responsible for Paul seeing David kissing me. It was just one of those things.

But I couldn't help feeling Fate had been most cruelly on Elva's side.

The days passed and I saw nothing more of Paul though I visited David a few times. More and more it seemed that that day on the island had never happened. Or, if it had, there must be some strange magic about the place which made people say things they didn't mean. My work became a drug which made me so tired that I slept well at night. I wasn't happy but I hoped that one day my pain and bewilderment might become a little less.

'I'm very pleased with the way you've settled into this ward, Nurse Marshall,' Sister told me when I'd been there about three weeks. She hesitated. 'I believe you had a little trouble before you came to Trent and I must congratulate you on putting it behind you so successfully.'

I left the office feeling ten feet high. It would take more, much more, than Sister's commendation to make me happy, but at least I had an inner satisfaction and that looked like being my lot.

Something else happened about then which gave me considerable pleasure. I was passing through the corridor near Medway one Sunday afternoon when I spotted Lucy among the waiting visitors. I knew she'd recently been discharged and I stopped to ask how she was getting on.

'I'm due to have the plaster off soon and Mr Greensmith thinks I shan't limp at all.' Her blue eyes shone. 'Only a few weeks ago I was so unhappy because I'd lost my boy friend and I thought one leg was going to be shorter than the other, and now everything's come right.'

'Everything?' I asked curiously.

'Well—yes, I hope so.' My question had obviously embarrassed her and she looked down at the bunch of sweet peas she was carrying. 'Are you wondering whom I'm going to visit? It's David actually—he asked me to come and see him after I was discharged. You—you don't mind?'

'Why on earth should I mind? David and I finished with each other long ago.' I smiled at her warmly. 'I'm very pleased you and he have got together.'

Someone had opened the ward doors and the people surged forward, taking Lucy with them. She flashed me a radiant glance over her shoulder and went on into the ward as I continued thoughtfully on my way.

I was really pleased about David and Lucy. She'd suit him far better than I had, with my impatience and quick temper. I didn't know whether they were serious or not but, whatever the outcome of this hospital friendship, I hoped neither of them would get hurt.

But though I was full of benevolence towards them, I couldn't help being envious. It was all so neat and just-what-the-doctor-ordered. There didn't seem any hope that my own life would ever become so tidy and well organised.

I hadn't even glimpsed Paul for some time and then I heard on the grapevine that he was away on holiday. I was beginning to feel I'd like a holiday myself but hadn't got anything lined up until the autumn. In the meantime I had to make do with my regular days off.

It was on one of these that I went into the city centre to do some shopping. The weather was hot and thundery and I wore a low-cut sleeveless dress yet was still too warm in the crowded streets.

I was wandering through one of the big stores when my attention was caught by some sort of a disturbance in the lingerie department. Somebody called out, 'Stand back and let her have some air!' and several people moved aside, giving me a view of a middle-aged woman lying on the carpet.

Acting entirely instinctively I went forward and spoke to the harassed floor manager.

'I'm a nurse—can I help?'

'I'd be glad if you would.' He turned to me

gratefully. 'She just collapsed without a word of warning. I hope it's just a faint but, of course, I haven't any medical knowledge and for all I know it could be a heart attack.'

I didn't pay much attention to his anxious babbling. I went down on my knees and felt for the woman's pulse, and at the same time examined her face for any tell-tale signs. She was naturally very pale and her lips had a bluish tinge which made me think she might have heart trouble.

Until then I had concentrated entirely on the medical aspect but as my patient began to show signs of coming round I suddenly realised that I had seen her before.

It was Lady Farnham, Paul's aunt.

I'd only met her once, on the night of the dance at Letherington Hall, but I was sure I wasn't mistaken, even though she'd looked very different then. As her eyelids flickered, I leaned over her and said very quietly, 'Lady Farnham— do you feel better now?'

Her eyes were staring straight into mine. 'I don't know you, do I?' she asked faintly.

'Not really.' I smiled at her and thought I saw a distinct likeness to Paul which I hadn't noticed before. 'But it doesn't matter—the important thing at the moment is that I'm a nurse.'

'Can't she get up now?' It was the floor manager again. 'It's really very inconvenient, having her lying here in the department. The ladies' powder room is quite handy—perhaps you could take her there?'

'In a moment. She mustn't be hurried.'

'I'm all right now.' She made a determined move. 'If you could help me—er—Nurse——'

I slipped my arm round her shoulders and helped her to sit up. She still looked very ill and I was more worried about her than I wanted her to know.

'Take it easy,' I urged. 'There's plenty of time.'

With the help of one of the sales girls I got Lady Farnham on to her feet. Between us we steadied her into the powder room and settled her in one of the comfortable chairs.

'Have you ever had a turn like this before?' I asked, thinking she might have some tablets in her handbag.

'Never. I haven't fainted since I broke my wrist at hockey when I was at school.'

'Then I can't prescribe anything except a glass of water. But I do think you should get home as soon as possible, as it's such a hot day. Did you drive yourself into Thorpevale?'

'I don't drive—which is fortunate in these circumstances. My husband lends me his chauffeur when I want to visit the city.' She looked keenly up at me. 'I still don't understand how you seem to know all about me. Unless—my nephew Paul brought some nurses to my charity ball, I remember. Were you one of those?'

'Yes.' The memory of that evening was too painful for me to dwell on and I hurried on. 'Where is the car parked? Is it far away?'

'In the cathedral car park. I—I don't know if I can walk that far, Nurse.' She looked at me appealingly, silently begging me to take charge.

'I'll ask the store to phone for a taxi. Sit here quietly and I'll be right back.'

I went with her in the taxi, of course, and saw her into her car. Just as I was going to close the door she suddenly caught my arm and held on to it.

'I suppose you're busy, Nurse? On duty or something?'

I shook my head. 'It's my day off.'

'But you've got social engagements, I expect?'

'N-no—nothing lined up. I thought of going to see my parents later on but——' I broke off abruptly, furious with myself for not being quicker-witted. I could now see quite plainly what was in her mind but it was too late.

'Then do let me persuade you to drive home with me and stay to lunch. For one thing, I shall feel much safer it you're with me. George——' she lowered her voice '—wouldn't be much good if I had another attack of faintness, and I should like to do something to repay you for your kindness. I'll send you back to Thorpevale by car.'

I thought of beautiful Letherington Hall and the cool shady park, and was tempted. It would be so different from the evening of the dance, I needn't think about it at all. Besides, I had no valid reason for not accepting.

'Thank you—that would be lovely,' I said politely, and got in beside Lady Farnham.

We spoke little on the drive and I was occupied in trying to control my rebellious thoughts. As we swept in through the elegant gateway and on towards the house I was plunged into such a tumult of emotion that I wished fervently I hadn't come.

What a fool I'd been to imagine the past could be brushed aside! It was there, pressing on me from all directions, rapidly becoming more real than the present.

I followed Lady Farnham into the house in a trance, washed my hands in a downstairs cloakroom and then went into the morning room where the table was laid for lunch.

'We always eat in here when we haven't many guests,' my hostess explained. 'The dining room is so ridiculously large.'

I almost said, 'Yes, I know—Paul told me,' but managed to bite the words back just in time.

I felt awkward and ill at ease all through the meal. Neither of us was hungry but I, at least, had to pretend. We were waited on by a man in a white jacket like the housemen wore but he had such a superior expression that he made me nervous. I was glad when we reached the cheese course and he vanished.

'I think I shall lie down for a little while,' Lady Farnham said, 'but I expect you'd like to go outside and——' She broke off abruptly as the door opened. 'Hullo, dear—I wasn't expecting you! I thought you were going to play tennis.'

I sat frozen in my seat. Although my back was towards the door I knew with a cold clear certainty that it wasn't Sir Michael who had come in. It was Paul.

He came round the table and looked blankly at me. After one quick glance I stared down at my plate.

'It was much too hot and we packed it in.' I could feel that his eyes were still on me but he went on addressing his aunt. 'I didn't know you were expecting a—a guest.'

Lady Farnham burst out into an over-dramatised account of what had happened. 'I'm so glad you've turned up, Paul, because you can entertain Joanne while I have a rest.'

He had listened gravely to her explanations and now said urgently, 'Perhaps you'll do what I've been suggesting for weeks—let the doctor give you a thorough overhaul.'

'Perhaps.' She smiled vaguely and stood up. 'I'll see what your uncle says.'

'He'll agree with me, that's for sure.' He opened the door for her and she went out.

We were alone.

'What would you like to do, Joanne?' Paul asked courteously. 'I could show you round the gardens if that appeals to you.'

'Thank you.' I still didn't dare to look at him. 'I expect it will be cooler outside.'

He led the way down a corridor and opened a side door. We crossed the terrace and went down some steps, coming eventually to great beds of roses and a wide herbaceous border.

'Do you really want to see the gardens?' He turned his head and looked down at me as I walked silently at his side.

'No,' I said flatly. And suddenly, without the slightest warning, I felt my temper rising. 'There's something I want far more than looking at—at a lot of flowers, no matter how beautiful they are.' I took a deep breath and whipped up my anger. 'I want to know why you've been ignoring me all this time after—after saying what you did when we were on the island. I like to know where I am with people——'

'So do I,' Paul interrupted. 'You said things on the island, too, Joanne, and I was fool enough to believe you meant them. And then, as soon as you knew David's leg was to be amputated you were back with him, and I'm darned sure it wasn't just out of pity.'

I stood still in the blazing sunshine and very nearly stamped my foot. 'But you practically told me to keep on with David for a while—you said we must wait until he was better before we told him about—about us.'

'Because I knew amputation was a possibility.'

'I thought that was it. And I did what you said though not only for that reason. I'd have kept it up anyway while he was so distressed about losing his leg.'

'He reacted to that very well,' Paul said, 'both physically and mentally. But you still went on being his girl friend—I saw you kissing.'

For some reason my anger had all evaporated. I said drearily, 'I don't suppose you'll understand but that was just a—an ordinary kiss, to show there was no ill feeling and all that. David and I decided we'd had enough of each other when I left Medway. He's got a new girl friend now—Lucy.'

'*Lucy?*' He seemed utterly amazed.

'That's what I said.'

We stood there silently in the quiet garden, where even the birds seemed too hot to sing, and there was no sound except the tops of the trees stirring in a slight breeze. Had I really heard nightingales the last time I was at Letherington Hall? There was certainly no song of joy in my heart now.

Suddenly Paul spoke.

'Do you really want us both to get sunstroke, Joanne? We shall be much more comfortable if we move over to that arbour cut into the yew hedge.'

He touched my hand tentatively and I offered no resistance. Together we entered the cool dark alcove and Paul's grip suddenly tightened.

'Why didn't you tell me all this before, Joanne? *Why?*'

'You didn't ask me, and you were so strange and withdrawn that time we met by chance near the tennis courts, I—I thought——' I choked and couldn't finish the sentence.

'I was worried about the amputation and very disturbed because I'd let the boss down the night before by being late back. You'll never know how much I wanted to take you in my arms but I couldn't—not with the operation going on at that moment. Besides, we had made that pact to keep away from each other until David was better.'

I could see it all now. We'd *both* been afraid to believe in the happenings on the island, neither had really trusted the other's love.

'Oh, Joanne darling——' Paul's voice shook. 'I've been so terribly unhappy.'

'I think,' I said hesitantly, 'that maybe we deserved to suffer for a little while. We shouldn't have behaved the way we did. If only one of us had had the courage to try and find out what had gone wrong, it could all have been sorted out before this.'

'Not to put too fine a point on it, we've been a

couple of idiots.' He put his arms round me and drew me close. 'But it's over now; we've got all the future before us. And perhaps because of this unhappy start we shall be all the more likely to guard and treasure our happiness in the days to come.'

I thought he was almost certainly right but I was in such a state of bliss that I couldn't think clearly at all, I could only *feel*. Paul's arms round me and his lips on mine, the thudding of his heart through his thin shirt and the close contact of his hard masculine body with mine—these were all I needed for perfect happiness.

At that moment the arbour at Letherington Hall seemed very near to heaven and I wouldn't have been surprised if I had heard nightingales singing—in the middle of the afternoon.

Doctor Nurse Romances

Don't miss
May's
other story of love and romance amid the pressure
and emotion of medical life.

HEAVEN IS GENTLE
by Betty Neels

Sister Eliza Proudfoot takes a job at Professor
Christian van Duyl's clinic and falls in love with him.
But then she finds he is already engaged to a placid
Dutch girl . . .

Order your copy today from your local paperback retailer.

Doctor Nurse Romances

and June's
stories of romantic relationships behind the scenes
of modern medical life are:

NURSE AT SEA
by Judith Worthy

Nurse Carole Wilson hopes a long sea voyage from
Australia to Britain will solve her emotional problems.
But when she finds the Ship's Surgeon is an old
boyfriend of hers, it is a case of out of the frying
pan into the fire . . .

THE UNWILLING LOVE
by Lucy Bowdler

Janice Colby starts her first job at Nootak — as nurse
to Eskimos — and has a warm welcome from everyone
except the handsome Mountie Philip Anson, who is as
chilly as the surroundings.

Order your copies today from your local paperback retailer.

Masquerade
Historical Romances

Intrigue excitement romance

THE FLAME STONE
by Kate Buchan

Charlotte's return to her childhood home in France was far from happy. In her absence her father had been branded a traitor, and Etienne de Chatigny — the man she loved — had married another girl. But why was the old Count so hated? And why did Etienne behave as though Charlotte had deserted *him?*

A GIFT FOR PAMELA
by Judy Turner

Lord Crispin O'Neill had forgotten to buy a gift for Miss Pamela Courtney, so he felt he had every reason for buying Peri — a most unusual slave girl — to repair his omission. Unfortunately, Miss Courtney loathed Peri on sight, and his lordship had to revise his plans in a hurry!

Look out for these titles in your local paperback shop from
8th May 1981

Take romance with you on your holiday.

Holiday time is almost here again. So look out for the special Mills & Boon Holiday Reading Pack.* Four new romances by four favourite authors. Attractive, smart, easy to pack and only £3.00.

*Available from 12th June.

Dakota Dreamin'
Janet Dailey

Forbidden Flame
Anne Mather

Devil Lover
Carole Mortimer

Gold to Remember
Mary Wibberley